Ghost Tree

Bill Deasy

velluminous

Published by Velluminous Press
www.velluminous.com

Copyright ©MMX Bill Deasy
www.billdeasy.com

The author asserts the moral right to be
identified as the author of this work.

ISBN: 978-1-905605-20-0

COVER DESIGN
HOLLY OLLIVANDER

GHOST TREE

Dedicated to the memory of Jon Hassler,
whose stories inspired me to tell a few of my own.
This one is a direct descendent.

Thanks, Jon.

1

"Impressive," Father Mike thought as his glance landed upon Monica Arnold, a woman he'd known since high school when she had represented the gold standard of beauty against which all other girls were measured, and who now sat in the seventh row of the funeral congregation. Monica wasn't Catholic, so she didn't attend Saint Luke's, which explained the priest's lack of awareness regarding the woman's continued luster. "Still gorgeous."

The ragtag volunteer choir of tone-challenged senior citizens dug into the responsorial psalm. Father Mike nudged his thoughts past Monica's triumph over kids, time, and an unappreciative husband and back to the reason they were there: Chet Howard had died. Chet Howard. *Chet freaking Howard.* How could that be possible?

He remembered their last encounter on a recent Sunday. Mike stopped by the Shake Shack for a burger after making his communion rounds to the parish shut-ins. Chet had been settling his check when Mike walked in.

"Great homily this morning," Chet had joked. "You really brought some things into focus for me."

Chet's wayward soul had become the last of their running jokes. Mike knew humor was his best hope of luring his old buddy back into the fold, and always went with it.

"I thought that was you, weeping in the last row. Glad I could be of some assistance, my son. You have ketchup on your chin, by the way."

Chet was back in the fold now, Mike supposed as he stood and walked to the lectern. God gets us all eventually, or something like that.

"I remember one night when Chet and I were in the ninth grade," Father Mike said, after reading the funeral's gospel passage. His hands gripped the podium. His eyes scanned the somber faces, as if he were addressing each of them individually, as he'd grown comfortable doing over twelve years of delivering homilies. "A Friday night, to be exact. We went to our very first high school dance. Now Chet and I weren't what you would call smooth with the ladies." This drew a titter from the captive audience. "But this was our chance to start fresh, we thought. Sure, most of our classmates at Pembrook High had been our classmates in grade school as well, but that didn't matter on that particular night. We were new men in a new place with new identities."

His dramatic pause was met with more soft laughter.

"There was one girl I'd always had a tremendous crush on. The kind of crush that causes you to forget basic skills – like speaking, walking, breathing." Father Mike glanced at Jane Taylor sitting red eyed in the very last row of the small church. Her nod assured him of what he already knew: she didn't mind him sharing this story. "Many of you might even know the object of my adolescent affection," he continued. "She's all grown up now, a fine upstanding citizen, and the manager of the coffee shop. She shall remain nameless."

More laughter. Everyone knew he was referring to Jane. Something was happening in the broken down barn of a church. People were realizing that although they were there to grieve and say goodbye to a dear friend, they were not there to do those things alone. They were members of something: a family, a community, a town.

"Now, girl X looked particularly fetching that night in her Jordache jeans and her Van Halen concert T-shirt. And, as I mentioned before, I was feeling braver than I had in quite some time. But I still couldn't muster the courage to ask her to dance. That's where Chet came in. Chet was the world's greatest cheerleader, the very model of moral support."

He shifted into a serviceable imitation of young Chet's voice.

"*'Dude, it's a different era, now,'* Chet said. *'We changed over the summer. You changed over the summer.'* He looked me up and down as if to verify his observation. *'Yeah, you're different all right,'* he confirmed. These were the skills that would later make him a legendary car salesman. He was selling me a better image of myself. And I bought it. *'And I just saw her looking over at you,'* Chet insisted. *'She's checking you out, dude.'* Chet was quite fond of the word 'dude' – even before it was fashionable.

"Long story short, I took the plunge. Thanks to Chet's rousing pep talk when the next slow song started I found the courage to walk up to the mystery girl and ask her to dance."

Father Mike paused. He knew he had them in the palm of his hand and that they all wanted to hear the end of the story. He held back a moment, then broke his own silence.

"You're wanting to know what happens next, aren't you?"

Nods and smiles all around.

"She told me to take a hike." After the laughter had died down he added, "Though she wasn't mean about it. Her answer was mercifully brief. 'No.'

"Crestfallen, I walked back to Chet and told him the sad story of the one-word rejection, and he did exactly what Chet always did, persuaded me to see it differently, to look for the silver lining, make lemonade from lemons, you supply the cliché. That's who Chet Howard was. He was a masterful revisionist who always saw the best in a situation. He was the kind of guy who might not take the bullet for you, but would tell you how cool it made you look, the moment you took it yourself. He was a true friend."

Father Mike stopped then. The story was all he'd prepared.

"I really don't know how to comfort you this morning … or myself, for that matter. To be honest, it hasn't sunk in. I still can't believe he's really gone." He ran his fingers through his short black hair and fought the tears that filled his eyes. "I will say this, though. I believe that Christ is in our suffering in exactly the same way He's in our joy. And I think, I pray, I hope that birth and death look much the same in God's eyes. Just as Chet was born into this world thirty-eight years ago, today he is born into eternity."

An hour after the funeral, Father Mike returned to Saint Luke's from the cemetery where they'd laid Chet in the ground. He would head over to Melissa Howard's house shortly, but needed a few minutes to himself. He treasured his time alone in the modest white rectangle of a church. Though he didn't actually believe that God was any more or less present there than in, say, a grocery store, the priest seemed better able to speak to Him in this threadbare house of worship, with its dozen small, square, stained-glass windows and its wooden pews seemingly designed to bring maximum discomfort.

He remembered the line from his homily about Christ being present in our suffering, and asked himself if he really believed that. He walked through the sacristy, gave a cursory look around to make sure that everything was in its proper place, then entered the sanctuary through the side door. All the while the questions continued. Did he have faith not so much in Christ but in the Church to which he'd devoted his adult life? Did he believe in his role as middleman between his congregation and God? Was he filled with the Spirit in the way he needed to be to fulfil his duties at Saint Luke's?

This train of thought led him to the one big question. The one he had not yet managed to voice but which he did then, silently, in the holy solitude of the sacred altar on which he'd consecrated ten thousand hosts: *Did he want to remain a priest?* He moved to his plush, red altar chair, the church's one extravagance, and sat down heavily, forcing himself to breathe more deeply as the weight of his doubt hit him like a bucket of bricks.

"Are you okay?"

The question came from a young girl he had not seen enter. She looked to be in her teens, and was pretty in a plain way; her freckles, brown hair, and brown eyes, a pleasant matched set that created an almost soothing effect.

"Yes," he replied, after recovering from the surprise of her presence. "I'm just a little emotional today."

"I was at the funeral," the girl replied. "I'm really sorry about your friend."

"Thank you."

"And I'm sorry to bother you," the friendly girl continued with an ease that impressed the priest. Too many teenagers talked to the floor and were incapable of looking adults in the eyes. This girl was different. "My name is Molly Faber. I'm a student at Harrison. A freshman."

"Good to meet you, Molly Faber. I'm Father Mike." He covered the ground between them and extended his right hand, which she accepted. "Is there something I can help you with?"

This was the aspect of his job that was never in doubt, those moments when another human being, sometimes a stranger, more often times not, reached out to him, and the two made a spiritual connection that did, indeed, feel sanctified by heaven.

"I think there is," the girl continued. "It's about your friend."

"Chet?"

She nodded then said, "I was in the room when he died. I volunteer at the hospital a couple of hours most weekdays. I talked a lot with Mister Howard when he first came in. Got to know him a little." She smiled, remembering. "I liked him. He was funny."

"This seems like a sit-down conversation," Father Mike interrupted.

They sat a few feet apart in the first pew.

"I stopped to visit him every day even after he went into the coma," she continued. "Just for a few minutes. I'd stand there. Maybe say something about my day or mention something in the news or whatever."

She paused.

"So I was there Thursday afternoon when all of a sudden I heard him whisper something. His eyes were still closed, and he didn't move or anything. It almost gave me a heart attack."

She paused. Mike was suddenly desperate to hear his friend's final words.

"What did he whisper, Molly?"

She leaned toward him.

"He whispered, *'Ghost Tree. Reunite the band.'*"

The strange, deathbed directive hovered in the air. Mike looked confused.

"He said what?"

"*'Ghost Tree. Reunite the band,'*" she repeated. "And then ... he died. Right then. I wasn't sure who to talk to about it. But then I came to the funeral and heard you talking, and I knew it was you."

"I'm glad you came, Molly," the shaken priest responded.

"Do you know anything about that band? Ghost Tree?"

"I was in it – if you can believe that one. A million years ago. I played bass. The girl I was talking about in my homily today was in it, too. Chet was our manager. We only played in public a handful of times."

"Must have left a big impression," Molly said.

"I guess so. I just can't quite get my head around it. I mean we hadn't talked about the band in years. Why would that have been his final thought?"

Molly broke the ensuing silence by standing to leave.

"I sure don't know, Father Mike, but I'm glad I found the right person," she said. "Hope I didn't bum you out."

She turned and headed for the front entrance.

Mike stopped her by saying her name.

"You didn't bum me out. Thank you for coming to me."

"Maybe I'll see you at the reunion show," she replied and then departed.

It was coincidence that brought Kenton Hall from New York to Chet Howard's funeral that weekend. Kenton's brother and sisters were throwing a surprise seventieth birthday party for their mom, and the curly-haired filmmaker's presence was one of the gifts. When he'd reached the house late Friday night, he was greeted by the news of Chet Howard's death. And though he was younger than Chet by six years and hadn't known him well, he liked him, and was more saddened by the announcement than he would have expected.

So Kenton was in Saint Luke's that morning and was there again in the early afternoon retrieving his cell phone, which must have slipped from his pocket during the service. He was just entering the building as Father Mike and his young visitor began their conversation. Sensing a need for privacy between them, he ducked into the shadows and waited.

Ghost Tree.

He hadn't heard that name in twenty years. When he was a kid, he'd spied on the band's rehearsals and was enthralled, to put it mildly, by the music they made. It was like nothing he had ever heard (granted, he was only twelve years old at the time.) The band may very well have been the reason he ended up pursuing a career in filmmaking. Their music had been cinematic, larger than life, and had left him in search of the movie to match it.

As the college girl left through one door and Father Mike through another, Kenton stood off to the side, an idea forming.

At 5:00 a.m. Monday morning, Jane Taylor pulled her long brown hair back into a ponytail, laced up her running shoes and walked out of the modest one-story house she'd called home for the past dozen years. Blue, her freakishly intelligent Australian cattle dog, spun around feverishly as Jane joined him in the front yard. The two had said their good mornings moments before, as they'd both awakened to the radio alarm. Blue was engaged now in his

traditional *I'm-about-to-go-running-with-the woman-that-I love-life-doesn't-get-any-better-than-this* dance. They trotted across the lawn and onto Route 29, in the direction of town.

As Jane found her pace she let her thoughts drift to Chet – big, silly, lovable Chet. She still couldn't compute the loss. Chet's presence in Pembrook was fundamental. He was a mountain of mirth, a brother for life, no matter how infrequently they saw each other. She loved him, plain and simple. Now he was gone.

Her sadness was deepened by the fact that their friendship had faded over the years. They'd moved in different circles. She was the coffee house maven, and he stuck to the steak and beer joints. But time could never erase the bond they'd forged in high school – Jane, Mike and Chet. Not a weekend went by in which they didn't do something together, if only just sitting around listening to music.

Mike's older brother had a vast record collection and it was almost like going to church when the three of them sampled his goods. There were the '70s crooners like Jackson Browne and James Taylor, edgier stuff like the Sex Pistols and the Violent Femmes, all of John Lennon's records – and, of course, every single Beatles song ever released. They also turned each other onto some unknown, up-and-coming artists like U2 and REM. Though Chet enjoyed the long nights of listening, it went deeper for Jane and Mike. It was like they were absorbing it all – the melodies, the production, the lyrics, the history.

Their shared love of music was what led to the highpoint of that golden era – Ghost Tree. The band was named for a towering old oak, famous in the town for its purported mystical properties. It was said that the spirits of all Pembrook citizens who passed away were housed there until their lives' remaining conflicts were resolved. It stood all alone in a field, not far from where Jane ran now – a field that was technically owned by the Mischelers but which had come to be considered community property over the years. Anyone was welcome to go there, and people often did – to forgive some sin or provide a final answer, thus granting a loved one flight.

Mike played bass, and Jane sang harmony and played rhythm

electric guitar. Nathan Booth, the singer, provided lead guitar. Jonathon Hilliard, now the Dean of Admissions at Harrison College, played piano and organ. Kenny Maxim drummed. Chet rounded out the equation as the band's fast-talking, overreaching manager. He booked their gigs and gave them rousing pep talks before each one – assuring, no, guaranteeing that each was a "stepping stone" on the path to fame and fortune. He'd insisted they were the next big thing. And for a few months, they were.

Jane rounded a bend with Blue angling beside her. The Hutchinson boy emerged atop his bike from his driveway fifty yards ahead, armed with a cloth sack, off to blaze his morning newspaper trail. The low, uneven line of Pembrook's modest "business district," barely cracked the dawn-lit sky.

Though the recently opened outlet mall a few miles away, strategically positioned next to the interstate ramps, had instantly become the small town's claim to fame, it would never be Pembrook, at least not for Jane. Pembrook would forever be the humble stretch of independent shops and restaurants that lined Broad Street, the slanting white-housed neighborhoods crowding around them, and the wide, gentle maze of country roads surrounding them. It would also be the idyllic, shimmering, white and green presence of the college that stood on the fringe of "downtown."

Jane and Blue picked up speed as Jane remembered Ghost Tree's final gig – a festival called Strawberry Days that was held each August in the heart of Pembrook. The few gigs preceding that one had generated a buzz, but their popularity solidified that day. Excitement surged like electricity through the large, beaming crowd. By the time the band hit the stage a little before sundown, you'd have thought it was a Rolling Stones show, not the seventh public appearance by a group of recent high school graduates who had a musical catalogue of nine original songs and one cover – *Peace, Love and Understanding*.

But then it all disappeared.

Jane fled to Pittsburgh. She heard Nathan went to Europe. Mike went to Erie, Jonathon stayed in Pembrook to attend Harrison,

Kenny took a job at Miller's Garage, and Chet went to work with his dad at the car dealership.

Ghost Tree was dead.

She saw Mike now, jogging in place at their traditional Monday morning meeting spot. His tall frame, black hair, and blue eyes gave him the look of a Kennedy. Jane envied his ardent religious faith. She could use some eternal, loving force to provide easy answers and comfort, right about now. But she'd given up on such notions years ago thanks to a pious, controlling father and a few too many philosophy books. She traded in the saccharine fairy tale she'd been given at birth, for a practical agnosticism.

"Top of the morning to you, Miss Taylor," Mike said in a horrible Irish brogue as he fell in step beside her. They continued down 29 away from town, instantly in rhythm. "And good morning to you as well, Blue," the tall priest said, also in dubious dialect, to the blue-and-gray-checkered dog.

"You seem chipper this morning."

"Totally faking it," Mike said. "I'm a mess."

"Glad to hear it. Me, too."

After a good five minutes in which the only sound to be heard on the tree-lined stretch of countryside was the pounding of their shoes on the smooth, black, two-lane asphalt, Mike said, "Something strange happened this weekend."

"You mean other than our friend kicking the bucket?"

"Yes," he said, "other than that."

He described his encounter with the college co-ed he'd met the afternoon of the funeral. Jane slowed their pace to a halt.

"Are you kidding me?" she asked. "Why the hell didn't you call me?"

"I thought I'd see you at Melissa's house," Mike said. "Then I got caught up with masses yesterday ... and just wasn't feeling like talking. Sorry."

"It's okay," Jane said more gently. "I don't know what I'm freaking out about. It's not like it's some giant breaking news story." She paused, gently biting her lower lip, then resumed running. Mike and Blue followed suit. "That's crazy though, Mike," she observed just after the first car she'd seen all morning passed on their left. "He was in a coma, for God's sake."

"Watch your language, Jane," Mike cautioned. "You wouldn't want anyone to mistake you for a believer."

"Has Chet even mentioned Ghost Tree to you in the past ten years?"

"No," Mike said. "Not that I can remember. Of course, I barely saw him."

"It's been bumming me out that we were so out of touch. How does that happen?"

"We grow up. We get lives. Losing touch seems to go with the territory."

"You and I have managed to maintain contact."

"That's just because I feel sorry for you," Mike said. "Never found a man. Living with a dog. Managing a coffee shop. I mean, how much more pathetic can you get?"

"I don't know," Jane said. "Sounds pretty good to me."

As they fell back into silence, Jane continued to contemplate their lost friend's strange, dying request.

"So what do you think?" she asked. "Should we do it? Should we reunite the band?"

"The band … is there even a band to reunite?"

"Well, we know where Jonathon is," Jane said. "He's busy being a Jesus freak up at Harrison. And Kenny's around and still playing out."

"I heard Nathan's back in the area," Mike interjected. "Living like a hermit in the mountains somewhere."

"Why didn't you tell me that?" Jane snapped.

"I don't know. I didn't think of it," Mike answered defensively. "I wasn't even sure it was true." They ran a few paces in silence before he continued. "And I can't imagine he'd be up for a reunion," he said. "I can't believe we're even talking about considering it. Are we talking about considering it? Aren't we like a million years old now? Who would even care if we got back together? I'm not even sure I can still play bass."

"Easy there, Skippy," Jane replied. "No one would care ... but we'd be fulfilling Chet's last wish. It seems pretty reasonable to me in a weird way. And you can still play bass. It's like riding a bike, or serving communion, or whatever the hell you do."

Mike laughed. "I just can't picture it."

"I can't either, really. But if you made some weird request on your death bed wouldn't you want me to make it happen?"

"I guess," Mike said.

"Let's consider it."

"Isn't that what we're doing?"

"Let's just keep considering it," she clarified.

The two friends, accompanied by a gray and blue-checkered dog, continued their run, considering for the better part of an hour.

Dr. Roy Kaufman appeared to be asleep. Edith Mathers wasn't falling for it, but had to admit it was a pretty convincing display. The snoring was subtle, believably arhythmic, and not the least bit hammy. There was even some drool involved.

Of course, this was the very end of the semester, and all of the students in the overflowing *Intro to Film* class had grown used to the gray-haired eccentric's clumsy theatrics. Finally, he burst to life, bellowing, "Time is up, as they say!" The students jumped in their seats, then started laughing. Edith smiled as she handed in the final exam of her freshman year at Harrison College and left the room – a free woman.

Moments later, she entered her stately dormitory and climbed its elegant staircase. She felt as good as she could ever remember feeling, even calling goodbye to the few girls she'd become acquainted with in the course of the year. She threw her stray belongings into a duffel bag, then started for the door. Before she could open it, though, she remembered the small, white container on the wooden dresser and went back to retrieve her pills.

The mountain man stood at the bathroom sink. He gripped the clean white porcelain and leaned toward the mirror. Smiling, he twisted the hot water faucet on with his steady left hand. He took the shaving cream and the new razor from the drugstore's paper bag, and set them on the back of the toilet, then splashed his cheeks with water and smeared on the weightless white foam. After holding the blade in the steaming current, he lifted it and shaved away the thick black beard. His clear, bright, gray eyes stared back at him in the mirror.

"There you are," he said, still smiling, then added:

"I am love."

"I am joy."

"I am light."

He repeated the three simple phrases aloud for several minutes, then proceeded to brush his teeth.

Monday, the late morning rush was severe due to the influx of parents and relatives in town for the day to retrieve Harrison students for the summer. Jane and her godson, Chuck, struggled to keep up with the flow.

Steerbucks Coffee Shop was conceived and owned by Pembrook's lone cattleman, Harry Compton. Believing that his town should bend to no trend, he outbid a mainstream coffee franchise for the space, then proceeded to borrow every aspect of said competitor's marketing and overall look-and-feel – while skewing each detail to match his own strong character and self-image.

In place of their frilly green-and-white circular queen emblem, Harry Compton's green-and-white circle featured a proud, snarling cow. And whereas the competition's merchandise racks cradled classy folk rock and soft jazz artists alongside fancy cups, games, and trinkets, his boasted the complete Merle Haggard and Way-lon Jennings, along with a dazzling array of lethal Bowie knives. The master stroke, though, was the subtle shift in name, which of-tentimes led visitors to believe they were in a café owned by the competition, giving Harry the feeling he was stealing "the man's" money – a feeling he liked very much.

Of course, Harry Compton was rarely there. In fact, it had been over two years since he set foot in the place. Consequently, towns-folk had come to perceive Steerbucks as belonging to Jane, if not in body then in spirit. Rarely did anyone call it Steerbucks anymore. It had become, simply, "Jane's."

Finally, by around two o'clock, things slowed down.

"Damn," Chuck said. "I don't think I've ever seen it so busy."

"You like this?" Jane asked referring to the CD she'd thrown on a few minutes before.

"Yeah, I do. Reminds me of someone from the 70s or something. Joni Mitchell?"

"Her name's Claire Jordan," Jane said. "Finbar sent it to me."

Dan Finbar was an old friend of Jane's who'd attended Harrison and been a regular performer at the coffee shop. He'd sent Jane the Claire Jordan disc along with a note saying, *"This girl is good. You should give her a gig."*

Jane agreed.

The song playing was as sad-sounding as anything Jane had heard in a long while. It suited her mood perfectly, a mood the morning throng had obscured but not dispelled. It was pure melancholy, which sprang not only from the loss of a friend but also from the re-surgence of memories she'd thought she had buried deeply enough to stay hidden. It was talk of a Ghost Tree reunion that did it. What the hell had she been thinking?

The entrance of two fresh-faced college girls interrupted Jane's brooding. The shorter one, whose straight brown hair fell to her slumped, tank-top strapped shoulders, came straight to Jane and introduced herself, expressing, somehow, that they were there for business, not pastries.

"Hi," she said, a little nervously. "My name's Edith. This is my friend, Molly."

"Hi," Molly chimed, her freckled face all smiles.

"We heard you might be needing some help here for the summer."

"You heard right. And my name's Jane, by the way. You guys aren't going home?"

"We're house sitting for the Krings," Edith said.

"They left for Italy already?" Jane asked.

The Krings were beloved by college kids and townies alike, easily bridging the gap that often existed between the two groups.

"Last night," Edith said.

"Is seven a.m. tomorrow too soon for you to start?"

"That would be awesome," Molly replied on behalf of both of them.

"Well, all right then. Be here tomorrow morning, and we'll see if you're Steerbucks material."

As the girls left, Old John, the town's ancient chess hustler, shuffled in, chuckling his raspy pipe-breath hello and giving Jane her first real smile of the day.

Van Morrison had done the trick, at least for the first forty-five minutes or so of Father Mike's impromptu drive to the monastery Monday afternoon. The bleary-eyed priest had successfully lost himself in the singer-songwriter's forty-year-old poetry. A song called *Cypress Avenue* was especially helpful. And yet, the clergyman's existential angst persisted – and was the reason he was going to Pittsburgh in the first place.

He crossed the Liberty Bridge then drove through a tunnel, returning his frazzled focus to the feeling that had awakened him far too early in the night, and kept him awake from that point forward.

Turning right just past the tunnel's end, a memory played. Mike was a junior at Mercyhurst; he'd overcome his antisocial tendencies and attended a fraternity party. The instant he arrived, he ran into a girl he knew from his *Economics 101* class. Her name was Betsy Kern. She had curly, black hair, freckles, and a few extra pounds. But she was friendly – and cute. She and Mike, each motivated by wallflower shyness, quickly struck up a conversation.

As Mike drank more and more of the free-flowing beer, his personality shifted into a new kind of friendliness, more like a talk-show host's than a mild-mannered college kid's. Before he was even aware of his own motivations he had invited Betsy out to enjoy the cool night air, and the two had walked through the deserted back lawn into a stand of tall trees.

Mike felt powerful. His words came easily. He was funny and comfortable in a role he had never played before – seducer. And soon both he and Betsy realized seduction was, in fact, his goal. In their drunkenness, they started talking about it, laughing.

Mike knew that he was not interested in starting a romantic relationship with her. He also knew that Betsy would gladly have called herself his girlfriend. He preyed upon her affection as he manufactured reassurances. The night ended with her performing oral sex on him on the dying autumn grass, the distance between them returning even before his release.

The next morning he awakened consumed with a shame unlike any he had ever experienced. His body ached with sadness, and he knew that he had used her, hurt her. He eventually managed to apologize to Betsy, and also shared his burden in confession. The relief he found there and his subsequent conversations with Father Valentine had been key reasons for his ultimate decision to join the priesthood.

As he pulled his dusty Toyota Camry into the monastery parking lot, he wondered about the authenticity of what he'd felt then. Did it – did *God* – really work that way? Had his sin really led him further from God's loving embrace, or had he been brainwashed to feel that way since birth – through a series of sacramental rites and a steady stream of information assuring him he was desperately in need of salvation? Was the Catholic Church just a giant master of Pavlovian psychology?

Father Bill O'Shea was forty-eight, ten years older than Father Mike – to the day. The two had met at a seminary in West Virginia where Bill taught Mike a course entitled *Theology and Politics in the Twentieth Century*. Father Bill had taken a special interest in Mike, dubbing the younger man an earlier version of himself. Their shared birth date sealed the deal. He became Mike's mentor, and they never went more than a week without talking or emailing.

"Michael," Father O'Shea bellowed in the doorway, and pulled the younger priest into his embrace. "So good to see you, my friend. Let's head back to my office, shall we?"

As they walked, exchanging small talk, Mike basked in the warmth of his tall, portly mentor's vast presence. Kindness surrounded the gentle bear of a man. The two friends continued side-by-side, down the quiet stone hall, then entered the building's less austere, carpeted, rear section. Father Bill's office door was the second one on the left. After grabbing them both a bottle of water from the small refrigerator tucked behind his desk, the older priest's smile changed to a more serious, concerned expression.

"Let's start with a prayer, Michael," Bill began. "Let's pray that the Holy Spirit infuses our conversation with light and grace, and brings peace to your heart. And that you'll find a voice here and now for whatever needs to be said."

After a moment of silence, they both murmured, "Amen."

"Now, what's got you so troubled? The angst is practically oozing from your pores. Is this about your friend? I was so sorry to hear about that."

"I don't know," Mike began, and then surprised himself by sharing the Betsy Kern story, and describing the way the sad encounter had made him feel.

"I know that feeling," Bill interrupted. "Every human being on the planet knows that feeling. We've all sinned. We're all sinners."

"I think that's part of what I'm wrestling with. That idea – that we're all sinners, fallen from grace. Is that really how God wants us to view ourselves? Were we made in His image or not? Maybe the whole sin and salvation motif was just a tool the early Church devised to keep people down and afraid. Is the Church really sanctioned by God, or was it invented by a bunch of 'believers' who thought they were doing the greater good?"

"Okay," Father Bill said, not rolling up his sleeves but sounding like he should have been. "I see where you're coming from here, Mike. Some fundamental questioning – you're having a theological crisis. And I don't mean to downplay it, but I'm relieved that's all it is. I was afraid you'd knocked up a parishioner, or fallen in love, or something really prickly." The priest paused, his smile returning for a moment. "The kind of crisis you're in is a gift. It's an opportunity for you to go deeper, to see and know more of the vast mystery that is God's love. And I know it hurts and it rips you apart when it's happening, but I promise you that you'll look back some day and be grateful for this temporary agony. I went through a very similar crisis at about your age.

"I also want to remind you of something you already know," Bill went on. "The ideas about God and the Church aren't God and the Church. God and the Church are in us, in people, not books or even the Bible. Your questions are all valid and worth a lot of hard consideration, but they're flimsy compared with those moments when you minister to the people in your parish ... .and actually do God's work. Does that make any sense?"

Back and forth they went, discussing the principles of Catholic theology. By the time Mike stood to leave, he'd been ushered, at least temporarily, to an internal ceasefire.

Driving back to Pembrook he returned his attention to the song he'd listened to on the way down. The lyric was truly perplexing, but the slow, plodding arrangement sucked Mike in every time. He thought about Father Bill, and about their conversation. Mike had been honest, of course, but only as honest as he had been with himself. It was only now, passing hills and fields that grew less populated with each green mile, that he let the final piece of the puzzle fall freely into his consciousness.

He was in love with Jane Taylor, and had been for twenty years.

2

On Monday morning, Kenton Hall walked twenty-three blocks from his midtown loft to the West Village. Walking was what he did when he wanted to induce solitary brainstorming. As each new project came up, either from his imagination or somebody else's, his first thought was, *"I need to take a walk."*

He had barely slept the night before, as the single cell of the idea that had appeared at Saint Luke's multiplied into a living, breathing organism. Passing a condemned church whose graffiti-filled walls announced the coming apocalypse, a plan began to form. He'd drive back to Pembrook tomorrow. He'd start from the outer fringes and work his way inward, interviewing the townsfolk, shaping the story like a sculptor shapes a statue.

The timing was perfect. He'd just finished a short film for the largest tennis-shoe manufacturer in America. They had wanted something artsy and inspirational about the great outdoors to usher in a new line of athletic equipment. And though it wasn't the art house premier some of his pieces received, the airing – on the giant screen at the company's national convention in Chicago – was thrilling, nonetheless. Truth be told, any work was good work in Kenton's humble opinion. That job was especially sweet for the hefty paycheck attached to it – a paycheck that would enable him to take a couple of weeks to chase the Ghost Tree thing down.

But first he needed a team, which was the ultimate point of his Monday morning expedition. He had called a writer named Susan Clawson the night before, and she'd agreed to meet with him. Susan had two excellent independent films under her belt as well as a slew of documentaries. She had also built a reputation for having the right touch storyboarding music videos, which was how they'd met a couple of years before – collaborating on a video for an independent band called *Sophocles' Soul*. Susan had conceived the story, and Kenton had brought it to life on film. They had worked well together, and though they hadn't reconnected since, he'd kept her in the back of his mind as an artist with whom he would like to work again. He sensed that Susan was the ideal partner for the type of documentary he was envisioning. It didn't hurt that she seemed ideal in every other way as well.

He found her number on a modest Charles Street brownstone and scanned the buzzer directory for her name.

"Hello?"

He liked her voice – a tumbler of fine whiskey with just a hint of sandpaper at the bottom.

"Do you ever feel like America is disappearing?"

"Sometimes."

"Me, too."

"I'll be right down."

He remembered her as being distinctly un-superficial, seeming to draw everyone straight past pleasantries and into the real stuff of life. Hence, his direct assault.

"There's this thing, a magical thing, that those of us who are old enough to remember, remember, but those who are too young, don't."

They walked along Charles Street with no apparent destination. Kenton had already worked through the hard process of acknowledging, then ignoring, Susan's beauty. No easy task. It helped that she was not only in a different league than he was, she was in a different universe altogether.

Kenton was 5'7" on a good day, with bespectacled eyes and hair that had not been combed in over a decade. She, on the other hand, was cover girl stunning: tall and sleek with angled cheekbones and jet-black hair. But her real beauty came from the way she didn't seem to know that she was beautiful.

"It's a magical thing that predates Facebook and YouTube and MySpace, and cell phones and digital technology – in that way it's as indie and pure as anything ever could be."

He kept his eyes straight ahead and forced himself to act as though they walked and talked like this every day. And what a day it was, each block more bathed in sunlight than the one before. Springtime in New York.

"I don't even know exactly what the magical thing is," he contin-ued. "I guess it's different for everyone. For me, it was music. But music on your own terms, in your own world, when you feel like you're the only person they're playing for – and that makes it more powerful or something."

"I'm with you so far," Susan said in response to his hesitation. "At least I think I am. I've been thinking about that kind of stuff lately, too. I've been thinking weird shit like how the next genera-tion won't know who Dean Martin or Sandy Duncan or Mary Tyler Moore or Laverne and Shirley were – which probably isn't exactly what you're talking about … but it seems to relate. I don't know … I guess each generation watches certain things disappear. But since our generation has ushered in the total explosion of information technology, the disappearance seems more final or something."

"I never thought of it that way, but I think that makes a lot of sense," Kenton said as they crossed the West Side Highway and stood beside the Hudson River. "And it might be why I'm getting such a strong feeling about the idea I want to talk to you about, and why I think we could make something cool together."

In some hidden corner of his mind, he understood that his last sentence might have two meanings – if it weren't for the whole sep-arate universe thing. Luckily for him, she didn't seem to mind that he was an ambassador from the planet Nerdroid – a punk version of Woody Allen.

"I was home this weekend," he continued.

"Where's home?"

"Small town in Pennsylvania called Pembrook. It's the kind of place that doesn't change much. Main Street cluttered with quaint old shops; small family-run businesses eking it out year after year. There's a college there that helps keep some life in the place – and they just threw up an outlet mall close to the nearest interstate, which kind of revitalized the town a bit. Mostly, though, it's the same as it ever was."

"Talking Heads, *Once in a Lifetime*," she free-associated.

"Exactly."

He went on to tell her about his mom's birthday, Chet Howard's funeral, his unexpected return to Saint Luke's, and the conversation he overheard there.

"The girl was the only one in the room with Chet when he died. Apparently he had some miracle moment and whispered something just before his final breath."

Kenton felt Susan leaning forward – if not physically, psychologically.

"Ghost Tree. Reunite the band." He let the words hang there.

"What's Ghost Tree?" she asked on cue.

"They were a band that was together in Pembrook one summer twenty years ago. I was twelve at the time. I used to run out to Berg's farm to spy on their rehearsals every night. They were awesome. Maybe I'm crazy, but in my memory they're right up there in terms of ground-breaking coolness. The lead singer, Nathan Booth, had this amazing voice, and the whole sound just kind of put you under a spell or something.

"I think we should do a documentary about getting them back together. We use the deathbed request as a hook and run from there. I know things like this have been done with bands that were famous, but I've never seen anything about an unknown band from an anonymous small town. Something that would reflect the real America, give people a glimpse at themselves and their pasts. If we play it just right, we could suck them into the drama of the band

and the mystery around why they broke up. I never understood it. After they played a few shows, people were going ape-shit over them, and then they just stopped. I want to know why. And I want to see if I can get them to play together one more time, to honor Chet's wish."

"What would it be?" she asked. "Like a feature film documentary type thing, or a reality show to pitch to a network?"

"I don't know," Kenton said. "I just know there's something there, and I have this weird feeling that you could help me bring it to light, find the right story to tell ... or stories."

He took his iPod from a shirt pocket and handed her the tiny speakers, which she obediently placed in her ears.

"Check it out," he said. "I had a tape from one of their shows. I converted it to disk last night, and threw it onto my iPod. This is one of my favorite songs."

He did his best not to watch her as she listened. He gazed out over the river and let the ideas run through his head. He saw the colorful cast of characters from the story of his life, and instinctively knew which ones might show him the way. He wondered to himself if a Ghost Tree reunion was even possible. Last he heard, Nathan Booth was living down south somewhere. And Mike Collins was a priest now – were priests even allowed to play rock and roll? His thoughts were interrupted by the sound of Susan Clawson's voice.

"Wow," was all she said. "Count me in."

Nathan Booth sat on a wooden chair by a square wooden table in his mountain cabin. His laptop computer gleamed before him. It was booted up, and functioning as a recording studio. He held a black, Martin acoustic guitar, and music played through his headphones – headphones that served also to keep his long black hair out of his face. An expensive microphone hovered near the instrument's sound hole. He played a simple melody over and over. As he sat still, allowing the final note to ring its way to silence, he heard a knocking at the front door.

"Congratulations," Nathan said in his thin, reedy drawl, "you're my very first visitor." Mike Collins smiled from the top of the entrance steps, dressed in jeans and a faded blue T-shirt. "Thought you were supposed to be a priest or something."

"This place is awesome," Mike observed as he entered, their hands clasping and releasing. They paused as Mike glanced around the cabin's interior with its deceptively high ceiling and each side more window than wall. "Who built it?"

"Me."

"Wow. That's impressive, man. I have trouble building gingerbread houses at the parish bazaar each Christmas."

They stepped farther into the house. Nathan reached for the guitar he'd left propped against the table, and placed it in its stand. "You want coffee?" he asked. "It'll have to be black. I'm fresh out of milk and sugar."

"Works for me."

Nathan went to the half-filled pot by the kitchen sink and poured their cups of coffee before leading the way onto the elevated back porch.

"I'm glad to see you're still making music. I was afraid you might have turned into a stockbroker or something." Side by side, they sat at the top of the stairs that led down into the cabin's backyard, which bled green and gold into the massive valley below. "It's like paradise up here."

"Something like that."

"Man, Nathan, you don't look a day older."

"Neither do you."

"I sure feel older," Mike confessed. "So give me the Reader's Digest version of the last twenty years."

"The first thing I did was join the army, if you can believe that one."

"The army? I didn't even know you were considering that."

"I didn't either," Nathan said. "It was my dad's idea ... thought it might help me find some direction. Last advice I took from him."

"Then what?"

"Hitchhiked all over. Lived a million places. Played music here and there. Nothing too exciting."

"Are you kidding me? To a guy who's spent his adult life living in a rectory it sounds like James Bond."

Two squirrels skirmished their way up and down the long, knotted trunk of the nearest tree. A steady breeze made the scene before them look slightly tilted.

"So what brought you back?"

"Just a feeling I guess," Nathan said.

"Chet Howard died last week," Mike said. "I wasn't sure you would have heard about it out here."

"Chet? Chet died?"

"Last Thursday. Heart attack. He was in pretty horrible shape. I mean he ate and drank a ton. Never exercised. Still a shock, though."

"Sorry, Mike," Nathan said. "I know you guys were pretty tight."

"Yeah," Mike agreed. "We were."

Nathan remembered the very last Ghost Tree show. At one point during the set, he'd looked to the side of the stage and seen Chet dancing. Their eyes had met and they'd smiled at each other. It was easily their most intimate moment.

"Jane, Chet and I were pretty much the Three Musketeers all through high school."

"Jane still around?" Nathan asked.

"Never left ... except for that summer. She runs the coffee shop in town."

"Jane Taylor," Nathan said, the words a soft path back through time. He briefly recalled Jane's abrupt departure after their last show – the departure that had, in a way, led him into the military and on through the odd journey that followed.

"Well, I better be getting back," Mike said, standing. "There are souls that need saving."

Nathan walked him around to the front of the house.

"Good to see you, Mike. Thanks for letting me know about Chet."

Nathan watched as Mike's car disappeared down the narrow dirt road. He stood for a while, remembering the eighteen-year-old versions of Jane, Chet and Mike. He smiled, kicked a rock, then went back inside.

When Mike got far enough down the mountain to regain cell reception, he called Jane at work.

"You what?" she yelled, after hearing of his visit to Nathan Booth.

"I went to tell Nathan about Chet."

"Are you kidding me?"

"No, I'm not kidding you. What's the big deal?"

He heard her give instructions to someone involving napkins and storage rooms. "Oh, I don't know, Mike," she replied when her attention returned. She sounded exasperated. "Don't even listen to me. I'm a moron. How'd you find him?"

"I went all Sherlock Holmes on his ass and called an old neighbor of his. And you are a bit of a moron," he agreed. "I'll stop by there in a bit, to try and smarten you up a little."

"Give it an hour," she said. "Should be quiet here then. Right now we're kind of slammed … and I'm training two new kids."

"See you in an hour, *mo*-ron," he replied with an awful southern twang.

As Mike continued his drive back to town, he thought about how little Nathan had changed. It was amazing, really. No thinning hair, no waistline paunch, no facial creases. Of course, Mike had none of those things either, but with Nathan the sense of continuity between then and now went deeper; it was as if the intervening years hadn't touched him. He still carried the same sense of serene detachment. He was still effortlessly cool in the most timeless, rock-and-roll sense of the word.

Mike, on the other hand, had changed: if not physically, then in other ways. He was more serious. He didn't laugh as much. He felt fatigued by life and the burdens his vocation forced him to carry with people. Those shared burdens were a gift, he knew, but they could still take a toll.

"I've turned into Father Mike," he thought to himself. "Nathan is still Nathan."

Instead of taking the left that would lead him to Jane's, Mike turned right on Highway 29. He had some time to kill and decided to fill it with a short trip down memory lane. In ten minutes, he was pulling up the long dirt lane that led up to Berg's farm. Ron and his wife would be at the junkyard, Mike knew, but they wouldn't mind Mike paying a visit in their absence.

The barn was wide open. Ron's Hammond organ and ancient sound equipment were still set up. The scene looked pretty much exactly as it had on summer nights all those years ago. The same giant wooden wagon wheel still hung suspended in lieu of a ceiling fan; the same grimed-over dime store paintings adorned the dusty walls. Mike breathed in deeply. The same sweet smell of grass, hope, and summer filled his lungs.

He could see them all as they'd been then, forming an imperfect circle. Jonathon, sometimes at his electric piano, sometimes at the organ, his kind brown eyes studying the others for musical road signs. Kenny Maxim, smiling behind the drums, reining them in with a grasp of the pocket that surpassed his years, and occasional bursts of inspired percussive insanity. Nathan, standing at the microphone, kissing it lightly as he set out on his nightly quest for lost words and hidden melodies, his sleek black telecaster shining at his waist. Jane, holding her uncle's bright red Rickenbacker, gazing at Nathan as if he were the captain and she his loyal-to-the-end first mate.

The time the band had spent in this barn was as holy and blessed as any Mike had spent anywhere. Mike didn't feel very holy or blessed today, though. He felt like the overwhelmed high school kid he'd been back then, and winced as he realized that it was his ancient, petty, immature jealousy that had kept him from sharing Chet Howard's final wish with Nathan Booth.

"Decaf, right?" Edith asked as she reached across the counter and retrieved Old John's empty cup.

"Why, yes," the stout old man replied. "If I have even a sip of the leaded, I'm up all night." He paused and looked at the wall as if there were a movie playing upon it. "It's so strange. I can't seem to stop thinking about an old friend of mine today. This fellow was a student at Harrison many years ago." Edith placed her only customer's freshly-filled cup back on the counter in front of his folded, age-spotted hands. "His name was Ransom Seaborn," John continued, after he'd murmured his thanks.

"That's the craziest name I ever heard." Molly, back from a bathroom break, had just rejoined Edith behind the counter. "Ransom Seahorn?"

"No, no, no, my dear. Sea-*born*."

"That's even crazier."

"He was shy and brilliant."

"Kind of like me," Molly joked loudly. "I'm shy and brilliant. Right, Edith?"

"And he was a bit of a minimalist when it came to conversation," John added. "Sadly, when I met Ransom, who was only twenty at the time, he was already not long for this world."

"What happened to him?" Edith asked.

"The poor fellow killed himself, I'm sorry to say."

Edith's memory flashed on her own suicide attempt, which had taken place early in her high school career. She wondered if perhaps the old man was psychic. His smile faded, but only momentarily.

"He was one hell of a chess player, though, pardon my French. Skilled beyond his age. In all my years of playing, he's the only one who ever beat me more than once. Of course," he added with a chuckle, "I usually steer clear of anyone I don't know I can take."

"What's this nonsense you're feeding my new employees?" Jane asked as she took a seat on the customer side of the counter.

"I was just remembering an old friend."

"Ransom Seafoam," Molly said, laughing.

"You can take off," Jane said to Edith.

"Cool," Edith replied.

Jane's faint freckles and green eyes gave her a pure, effortless, all-American beauty. The dimples didn't hurt, either. Molly seemed to snatch the thought straight out of Edith's brain.

"Where did you get those dimple, Jane? They're almost not fair."

"I really don't know," Jane replied with a laugh. "Can you stay until three when Chuck comes, Molly?"

"Sure thing."

"It was nice talking with you, Old John," Edith said, touching her new friend's forearm. "See you tomorrow?"

"The good Lord willing and if the creek don't rise," he replied.

Jane saw Mike enter the coffee shop and started toward him, calling back to Molly who was organizing inventory. "Can you cover the counter for me when you're done back there? Should be quiet for a while."

"Sure thing," Molly replied.

Edith and Molly had been coffee shop savants, quickly picking up on every caffeinated drink concoction Jane could throw at them, and mastering the convoluted cash register with ease. They even acted interested when Jane filled them in on Steerbuck's comical origin.

Jane met Mike at the café's halfway point.

"Have a seat," she said, taking one herself at the nearest table. "Need anything?"

"I'm all set," he replied, which was a running joke between them. Mike had worked one summer doing telemarketing and determined that "I'm all set" was the foolproof response, guaranteed to derail even the most mercenary of telemarketers.

"So tell me everything," Jane urged, whispering slightly and leaning closer as if they were surrounded by dozens of potential eavesdroppers. "He's fat and bald, I hope?"

"No such luck," Mike said. "It was actually kind of unsettling how much he looks exactly like he looked before."

"Shit," Jane said. "I was afraid you might say something like that."

"Would you watch your language, please? I'm a priest."

"So what else? Tell me everything."

"Could you act any more like a schoolgirl, Jane?"

"You wouldn't understand," she said finally. "It's a girl thing."

"Give me a break," Mike replied. "It's not a girl thing; it's a Jane thing."

"Did you mention Chet's request?"

"No," Mike said. "For some reason, I didn't. I think I just started to feel like it was all sort of ridiculous. I suddenly couldn't imagine myself in a million years strapping on a bass and performing in front of people – not that I think anyone would come – and so I didn't even give it words."

"Guess that makes sense," she said. "Although … you were out there with him … I'm still kind of surprised you didn't mention it."

"Can you picture it? Can you actually picture us playing again?"

"No," she said. "I guess I really can't."

"So what are we going to do?" Mike asked. "Are we going to ignore our friend's dying wish?"

Jane paused, frowned, smiled, looked away. "No, Mike. I don't think we are, are we?"

Mandy Lomax was short, squat, and very butch. You'd have thought for sure she was a lesbian if she wasn't always talking about finding a husband and making babies. And even then, you would still have thought she was a lesbian. Susan Clawson didn't care either way, of course. Mandy was the best videographer Susan knew, and Susan was thrilled to have gotten her on such short notice.

The project already had the feeling of serendipity. She had just been thinking about Kenton Hall – remembering how well they'd worked together and how quickly she'd come to trust his instincts and enjoy his quirky intensity. Susan had just received a much larger-than-expected check for her first novel, and was temporarily free and clear … looking for a new adventure when Kenton showed up. Funny how life worked when you let it.

The Cloverleaf Motel, located exactly three miles from the heart of Pembrook and three miles from the Outlets Mall Mega Complex, did not just have one or two vacancies – it had twenty-four of them, a number that matched its room total. So Susan had no problem commandeering rooms for herself and her two colleagues.

The old Italian man who checked them in eyed their equipment suspiciously. "You're not going to be doing anything kinky in these rooms are you?"

Susan laughed, tickled by the gray-haired man's bluntness. "Nothing planned," she said.

"Well, that's good. I run a clean establishment here. Don't want anyone making any sex tapes or anything like that. My name is Lou, by the way. I own this place."

"My name is Susan, Lou – and we'll do our best not to discredit your establishment in any way."

"How long have you been here, Lou?" Kenton asked as he joined Susan at the counter.

"Who's this guy?"

It seemed that because Lou and Susan had spoken first, all roads to him would pass through her. Susan loved this man. She eyed Kenton suspiciously. "Kenton Hall," she said. "You never heard of him?"

"Never heard of him."

"I grew up here," Kenton said, seemingly oblivious to the quickly-forming group dynamic, and to Susan's silliness.

"I been here since 1989," Lou said, trusting by association.

"Nice to meet you," Kenton said.

"Who's she?" Lou nodded in the direction of Mandy, who was holding a small video camera in her right hand and scanning it across the dreary office.

"That's Mandy," Susan said, not in the least bit discouraging her role as point person. "She's our camera woman."

"A camera woman?" he asked. "I've never heard of such a thing."

"They're all over the place," Susan said. "Say hi, Mandy."

"Hi."

"Is she shooting me?"

"I think she might be, Lou. Are you shooting him, Mandy?"

"Just making sure that terrible turnpike didn't break anything."

Lou handed Susan three keys across the counter, each one affixed to a plastic, brown cloverleaf. "You need me for anything, any time of the day or night, just come down here and hit the buzzer." The portly motel manager cast his lazy left eye at Kenton, clearly suspicious of the party's only male. "I'm always here."

"Good to know," Susan said. "It's really good meeting you, Lou."

"You can call me on the phone, too," he called as they made a move for the door. "Just press zero."

"Thanks, Lou," Susan called back. "Got it!"

Half an hour later, *Mystic Light* played on the stereo in Kenton's car. Susan had made a CD of the song repeated twelve times in a row. They had just made a stop at the Ghost Tree field. Susan was grateful to have such a strong central symbol for their story. The tree was impressive, to say the least. They drove now along Rt. 29, the two-lane that led into Pembrook.

She asked for Mandy's hand-held and turned down the music as she pointed the camera at Kenton. "So why are we here in Pembrook, Pennsylvania, Kenton Hall?"

"We're here to solve a mystery," Kenton said. "Twenty years ago, when I was a boy growing up here, there was a band called 'Ghost Tree.'" He reached forward and turned up the volume momentarily. "That's one of their songs. You hear that? Still sounds good all these years later. They were only together for one summer, and they only played a handful of gigs. But they left a mark on everyone who saw them, especially me."

"But why now, Kenton?" Susan asked. "Why would you choose now to chase down a memory of a band no one ever heard of ... a band you saw a few times twenty years ago?"

"Like I said. We're here to solve a mystery. Let's just leave it at that for the moment."

Onward they drove, past the Boot Box and Katie's Corner, the American Legion and Grace Methodist, the three-pump Gulf station and Curves aerobics studio, canvassing the area while Kenton delivered a running commentary on what they were seeing.

"I went to grade school there – and the high school's right beside it. There's Saint Luke's. That's where I overheard Father Mike and the college girl. There's the Guthrie." He pointed at the classic-looking theatre marquee leaning proudly above the entrance. "Pizza House. Ithen's. Seriously, nothing ever really changes here."

For over an hour they drove, talking while Susan drank it all in. Small town America. She reflected on what that phrase meant, and how a million bands like Ghost Tree had sprung up in towns like Pembrook since Elvis first shook those crazy hips of his.

Was Ghost Tree any different than all the others? Were they as special as Kenton thought they were? She was inclined to answer both of these questions in the affirmative, based on gut instinct, and on the fact that the song that continued to loop on the car stereo had only grown more pleasing to her ears with each play. She sang along softly as they pulled into the Pembrook Diner for an early dinner.

Nathan walked the thin, buried path to a stream about a mile from his home. He carried his guitar in his right hand and his camping gear on his back. He reached his spot and set up camp: pitched the tent, collected wood, hunkered down for the night. After he'd eaten a light dinner of chicken and rice and tidied the area up, he sat cross-legged outside his tent on a Navajo blanket he'd acquired in New Mexico many years before.

Darkness spread above him like black paint across the sky, and was perforated by a million sparks of brilliant starlight. He'd grown used to the magnificent canopy, but worked hard not to take it for granted. He sat utterly still and breathed in the cool night air. He focused on each breath, counting his way deeper and deeper into a state of blissful blankness.

Normally, entering thoughts were nudged away gently from his consciousness. This night, though, he let one stay. He saw Jane Taylor in his mind's eye as she had looked all those years ago, smiling, grooving to the music, leading them without even knowing she was leading them.

Nathan reached for the weathered brown notebook he'd placed in his bag. He'd found it in a box of his old belongings that his parents' neighbors had kept for him. His handwriting was a bridge through time that led him to that summer. After rehearsals, he'd sit in his bedroom and write the things he'd been thinking as they played, as well as whatever lyrics he'd managed to string together. It was mostly meaningless now – the babbling of a teenager desperate for flight.

He turned toward the back of the book and found a page that bore the heading "Mystic Light." He read the fading words.

> *I ain't seen no visions.*
> *Ain't like William Blake*
> *Ain't been moved to speak in tongues*
> *Or walk across a lake …*

He lifted the Martin gently from its case. He had it tuned to open C, and marveled at the way the first notes resonated in the night. He'd done this many times before – played music by himself out in the middle of nowhere, and it always gave him the sense that he was not a person at all, that he was in no way separated from his surroundings. The music reduced him to atoms and soul, and his voice above it was as natural as the wind.

With eyes closed, he chanted his way to ground that was familiar and yet still foreign. Finally, in this strange tuning he hadn't even known twenty years ago, he latched onto the chord progression and began to sing the words he had written in another lifetime.

This was the song that had told them they were a band ... they were Ghost Tree. This was the song they wanted to play again, the moment they finished it. *Mystic Light.* Nathan was surprised by how good it felt to sing the strange, old song, and knew that the search he had sung about back then had led him to this place and to this moment.

It was after midnight. An empty pizza box sat atop the motel room's lone dresser. *Mystic Light* piped through the small built-in speakers of Mandy's expensive laptop, which currently served as the project's editing suite. Kenton was pleasantly surprised by how deeply the music had hit both Susan and Mandy: they were instant Ghost Tree groupies. Mandy had taken to referring to Nathan as the future father of her children.

Susan leaned over Mandy's shoulder and thought out loud with them, her ignorance serving as her guide. "Would it be possible ..." was the phrase that seemed to start each sentence, and Mandy generally nodded in the affirmative, fingers ablaze atop the keypad. Something was already beginning to take shape.

As Kenton stared at the computer screen over Mandy's other shoulder, he remembered the story-of-her-life skeleton Susan had laid out for him the last time they worked together. Honor student, beauty queen (literally – pageants, tiaras, the whole nine yards), pothead, former pothead, writer extraordinaire. He'd filled in that last part, after reading everything of hers that he could find. The girl was good. And he was starting to glimpse her vision of the moment – a kind of music video for the Ghost Tree song – a project teaser of sorts.

The ghost tree itself, towering, alone and stark in the open field; then the scene from the road as they first entered town accompanied by the song's instrumental introduction, until Nathan's voice took over, singing with an ethereal quality that belied its strength, deepening the spell. Mandy had manufactured a grainy look that gave the video a low-tech timelessness. The unfolding scenes of the town seemed to flow from the song. It was perfect.

Kenton could feel what was happening, and he knew that Susan and Mandy felt it too. Smiling like fools in a seedy room at the Cloverleaf Motel, they were stumbling into something beautiful.

Father Mike hadn't set foot in the 'Landmark' in a decade or so, but he was there Tuesday with an itch to blow off some steam. The place was packed. Townies were engaged in a spontaneous celebration in honor of the college kid exodus.

Dollar Buds and the Allies' standard Tuesday performance only made the night more festive. Mike watched from his corner stool at the bar. He observed the raucous crowd and thought it felt more like the night before Thanksgiving than the second evening in an ordinary workweek. The spirit of the people in his hometown never ceased to amaze him.

Kenny Maxim sat behind his drum kit and counted the band into a cover of the Rolling Stones' *Sympathy For the Devil*. Mike felt the familiar combination of guilt and appreciation the song always produced: good old Catholic guilt. The six beers he'd consumed tipped the scale in favor of appreciation, and he sang along.

"Is this a sign of the Apocalypse or something?" The slurred question came from Larry Terk, two stools over. For lack of a better term, Larry was the town drunk, lost and loveable. The 'Landmark' was his headquarters. "A priest drinking beer at a bar singing *Sympathy For the Devil*. Can't be good."

Mike looked toward Kenny, noting that the drummer also looked very similar now to the boy he'd been twenty years before – more mature, yet not older, *per se*. Mike was sensing a trend here: Ghost Tree; Fountain of Youth. He glanced again at Larry Terk, who looked about sixty – but who was only half a dozen years older than Mike and Kenny.

Larry, clearly, had not been in Ghost Tree.

"Jesus Christ come heal me right here," Mike pleaded in his head. "Heal me right here in this ragged old bar among these good, lost people. Heal me here beside Larry Terk. Heal us both – Larry of the emptiness he keeps filling with booze, the hole that only you can fill. Me, of this ridiculous lovesickness I've ignored for so long. I gave myself to you, Christ – not to Jane. Can't you make that decision feel a little sturdier than it currently does?"

He was getting drunker. He felt it. He needed to watch himself. Word spread quickly through a small town. The Catholic priest getting drunk at the Landmark was notable. It would easily make the gossip line.

"It's probably a sign of something, Larry," Mike said finally in answer to Larry's query. "Everything's a sign of something, right?"

His delayed response reminded Mike of some fine theological point over which he'd waxed in the seminary. He couldn't quite recall what it was. Something about life itself being a sacrament.

"You hear they're making a movie here?" Larry asked.

A shot glass filled with whiskey had been placed at the side of the priest's right hand, which was perched upon the cash-littered bar. Mike barreled past his fleeting reservations, and downed the hard liquor with a squinty grimace. He smiled at the Miller Lite girl posed in a poster above the shelves of assorted cheap booze.

"No, Larry. I hadn't heard that."

If they were, in fact, in a slurring competition, Mike was making his move.

"Hey Mike," Kenny Maxim said above the din, falling onto the empty stool between the drunk and the priest. Come to think of it, Mike had noticed the music shift from live to jukebox.

"Larry was just telling me about a movie being made here," Mike said, striving for normal conversation against the backdrop of his growing sense of slipping down a dark dirt path.

"Kenton Hall," Kenny said.

Kenny was thin and freckled, and his hair was stringy and yellow and added to the impression that he was a comic book character come to life, the happy clown in a gang of troublesome yet funda-

mentally good-hearted teen-agers. Mike had always liked him immensely.

"I've always liked you immensely," Mike said.

"Right back at ya, Mike," the unfazed drummer replied. "Kenton's
here with some beautiful lady from New York. I mean, like, Cheryl
Tiegs beautiful."

"Did you just use Cheryl Tiegs as a cultural reference point?"
Mike asked. "She's got to be about seventy now."

"I always thought she was hot. They're making a movie about
Pembrook or something."

"Pembrook?" Mike asked. "Isn't that kind of like making a movie
about paint drying?"

Larry laughed. Kenny kept talking. "Fay served them dinner.
They interviewed her. She knows all about it."

Fay, Mike knew, was the beating-heart switchboard of the town
gossip line. She waitressed at the Diner in addition to working late
shifts at the Donut Shack.

"I saw 'em," Larry said. "Saw 'em standing at the corner of Broad
and Pine pointing their camera at something. Couldn't figure out
what the hell they were doing."

Mike suddenly felt sick. The whiskey was having a delayed reaction. He forced himself out of his chair and applied all of his
concentration to walking steadily from the bar to the door, toss-
ing a garbled "Gotta go" over his right shoulder. The moment he
was outside he stumbled down the steps, knelt, and vomited. The
retching was mercifully brief, and he was relieved to find no specta-
tors when he lifted his gaze up from the parking lot and stood.

"That feels better," he said, aloud, to no one.

He looked around as he got his bearings. The night was perfect.
So perfect, in fact, that for one beautiful moment Mike was pro-
foundly reassured of God's presence, and the weight on his heart
lifted. He thought he might even be able to fly, like a bat or a raven
through the eternal, mysterious night.

This childish notion was replaced by a memory. He saw himself
twenty years ago – a confused boy, no longer a boy, walking away

from a summer night rehearsal, overwhelmed by the magnitude of the feelings he owned but didn't understand. Walking and aching, the soft strands of Hammond organ piping through the barn walls behind him.

The weight returned.

3

Jonathon Hilliard was the Dean of Admissions at Harrison. As such, May was his easiest month. With one class graduating and another class locked in for the following September, there wasn't a whole lot going on.

Wednesday morning he called his secretary, Martha, to say he'd be working from home until after lunch. Unbeknownst to Martha, what this really meant was that he would be turning his stereo's volume knob as far to the right as it would go and playing the new John Doe CD he'd received from Amazon the day before.

John Doe was Jonathon's favorite. He couldn't say why exactly. It had something to do with an intangible quality he heard in the singer's unrefined voice. Openness, wildness, unpredictability, and vulnerability – all wrapped up in a loose, messy, magical musical package. He could tell with the first notes of the first song that the new one would stand proudly beside all the rest – just as Jonathon had known it would. He trusted his heroes.

Dressed in firmly-creased navy blue pants and an untucked, bright-white undershirt, he jumped around his study as if overtaken by demons. He couldn't help himself.

"Dad."

He waved his arms wildly, his short, wiry body gathering unsteady momentum, his bright red hair tight and unmoving against his head, which lolled and bobbed erratically. He was an airplane, a teenager, a spinning top. He smiled with his eyes closed as he fell deeper and deeper into the song.

"Dad."

He bumped into the bookcase. Several Encyclopedia volumes tumbled to the wooden floor, but he danced on, undeterred. The music stopped suddenly. His teenaged daughter, Samantha, stood laughing. Jonathon's three children were used to his bursts of music-induced physical exuberance but could, on occasion, still be amused by them.

"You scared the heck out of me, Sam."

"I tried yelling, but you didn't hear me. I need to show you something."

Slightly winded and with a thin sheen of sweat across his forehead, he followed her from the silenced room up to her second-floor bedroom. Her laptop was opened on her work desk, and a song was playing from it, a song that was vaguely familiar to Jonathon.

"Check this out," she said.

He looked at the screen and recognized his hometown flashing in seamless scenes before them.

"That's Pembrook," he said. "There's Saint Luke's. How the heck did you get this, Sam?"

"Karen just sent it to me."

"What is it?"

"A video on YouTube."

The most alarming realization, though, was not about the video's familiar scenery; it had to do with the organ being played on the accompanying song. It came courtesy of him, Jonathon Hilliard, twenty years ago. Somehow, miraculously it would seem, they were listening to his former band: Ghost Tree.

"That's me," he said. "That's my old band."

He couldn't stop shaking his head.

Mrs. Manella was a lifer. She had just finished an oldie but goodie from Genesis, and Mike had to hand it to her – the old girl could still deliver some scripture. He hoped he was half as lucid if, God forbid, he lasted to the ripe old age of ninety-three, as she had. As Mrs. Manella proceeded to lead the sparse group of midweek morning worshippers in the responsorial psalm, Mike, suffering his first hangover in years, imagined a man of his age worshipping God in some far away place, listening to passages from his holy book. A Hindu in India, a Muslim in Iraq – believing every bit as firmly as Mike believed.

Was it simply the luck of the draw that Mike was born into the true faith, while his counterparts went down their inherited blind alleyways? Couldn't they be asking the same thing about him? Was it arrogance on all of their parts to believe that their book was the true book; their perspective, the true perspective; their faith, the true faith? Was it more likely that they all had it right or they all had it wrong?

After the gospel passage, Mike said, "pillars of dust." That phrase had been kicking around in his brain for weeks. Sometimes, at the weekday masses, he'd throw out a fragment of an idea and see if it led anywhere. If it did, it would eventually end up at the heart of a Sunday homily. Now that he'd spoken the words aloud, he had no idea what to say next. "That phrase keeps coming to me lately," he tried. "Perhaps another way of saying it is 'mountains from mole hills,' though I'm not sure that has the poetic resonance of 'pillars of dust.' And priests, especially priests of Irish descent, are always looking for some good old poetic resonance."

His mouth was dry. He paused, and, with closed lips, tried manufacturing some saliva with his tongue. The effort was futile.

"Pillars of dust," he said again, still not knowing where he was going. "I think in many ways we all try and build our lives upon pillars of dust. Vanity. Maybe that's one. How do I look? What does everybody think of me? And if you go a little deeper with that one, why does everybody else seem happier, more successful, farther along the path to … you fill in the prize. We all throw heaps and heaps of energy into that kind of thinking until it becomes a giant pillar, which might look sturdy and durable, but which one strong wind will blow away.

"Or how about pride? Is that another one of them? Not the acceptable pride that comes from a legitimate accomplishment, like building a back deck on your house without the help of a professional ... builder ... person. Not that kind of quiet-satisfaction type pride. I'm talking about the harder-edged, *you hurt me and I can't forgive you* pride, the *I'm right and you're wrong come hell or high water* type. That's a pillar of dust if ever there was one.

"And how about flat-out prejudice? Maybe not the overt prejudice you see on display in documentaries about the civil rights movement, but a more invisible, menacing kind. The kind we barely even know is there – a low voice whispering in the backs of our minds that we're better, smarter, more deserving...

"You get where I'm going, right? All of these things, and a hundred others, pillars of dust upon which we all, me at the head of the line, build our lives."

He knew his weekday soul warriors weren't used to this long of a homily, and he needed to bring it to a close. He noticed Kenton Hall entering through the church's rear doors. Two women followed – one was tall and thin with curly black hair, the other was shorter and carried a video camera. All three of them wore jeans and T-shirts – the big city artistic types' uniform of choice, it seemed. Now he really needed to find his conclusion.

"What if instead of those pillars, we made different ones, pillars built around the lessons Christ taught us – lessons of compassion, mercy, forgiveness, in a word: love. Those are the pillars that can stand up to even the most severe weather, the most violent and unexpected wind gusts. Those are the pillars I encourage us all this morning to lay the stories of our lives upon."

"Stories of our lives," he thought as he left the pulpit. "Where the hell did that come from?" The whole thing sounded like platitudes even to Mike – especially to Mike – but he'd run out of steam. He barreled through the remainder of the liturgy and sent his loyal flock on its way.

"Hey, Kenton," he said when he met the trio in the center aisle. Mike always had the sense that there were strange and wonderful worlds being created behind Kenton's eyes. "Heard you were back in town ... again."

"Hi, Father Mike."

"You don't really want to call me Father, do you?"

"Sorry, Mike."

A social cloudiness surrounded Kenton, so that no one in his presence was ever sure whose turn it was to speak. Mike and the tall woman made an attempt at the same moment.

"I'm sorry," Mike said.

"I'm Susan Clawson. I'm a friend of Kenton's. This is Mandy Lomax."

Mike shook hands with them both, and they all looked at Kenton who seemed, as always, to be slightly perplexed.

"You guys mind if we talk outside?" Mike asked, then led them out into the bright, warm-morning sunlight. Summer was coming faster than usual. Mike glanced at the church and decided the doors needed some paint. Maybe he'd even go with a different color.

"So," Kenton began with trademark awkwardness, "I forgot my phone here after Chet's funeral, and when I came back for it I overheard your conversation with that girl. I heard what she said about Chet's last words. It got me thinking about Ghost Tree and about music and about Pembrook and about a hundred different things. I thought it would be fun to come and see if we could make it happen."

"Make what happen?" Mike asked.

"A reunion," Susan said with a smile that could embarrass the sun. "We came here to make a documentary about getting your old band back together."

"A reunion?" he said softly.

"Is that lead singer as beautiful as he sounds?" the short one,

Mandy, asked. Mike hadn't noticed that she was documenting the whole exchange. "Can't wait to track him down."

"You okay with Mandy taping this?" Kenton asked.

"What?"

Mike couldn't seem to focus. The hangover and the surreal quality of the 'interview' in which he suddenly found himself were throwing him off of his game – way off.

"Is this okay? Mandy pretty much records everything, and we sift through it all later to see what's what."

"To be honest with you, Kenton, I need to think about this a little. I'm not sure how I feel about anything right now … let alone a Ghost Tree reunion. You're catching me at a strange time."

"Do you think we could set up a time just to talk to you about the band and about what you remember from back then?" This came from Susan – the friendly, dazzling one.

Mike nodded. "I don't see why not. I'm just a little out of it today."

"That's cool," Kenton said. "Is there a time that works for you?"

"How about ten a.m. tomorrow? Let's meet back here."

Mike shook each of their hands again and watched as they walked to their car. Mandy paused to shoot some footage of the church and, Mike supposed, of him standing by the church. All in all, he couldn't have asked for a stranger start to his day.

"I'd do him."

Susan made this statement as Kenton backed his car out of the Saint Luke's parking lot.

"Me, too," Mandy said. "Handsome priests turn me on. I would totally do him."

"What?"

"Father Mike," Susan said. "He's a hottie."

"Really?"

"Really," Mandy said. "I'm a sucker for the blue-eyes-black-hair combination."

"Father Mike is one of the best people I've ever known," Kenton said. "Even though he was six years older than me, he always treated me like I was his friend. He never talked down to me. And I know he's really helped my sister out. She goes to Saint Luke's and had a rocky marriage and an even worse divorce, and Mike kind of guided her through. My mom thinks he walks on water."

"I like him, too," Susan said. "That is one likeable priest. Think he'll come around for us?"

"He acted like he wasn't even aware of the death wish thing," Mandy said.

"I really couldn't get a feel for it," Kenton said. "He seemed a little off to me. Maybe he's still mourning. I think the whole town is kind of hung over from Chet dying. Chet had a pretty massive personality. Left a big space."

"Well, maybe our movie can help fill it," Susan said. "How's that for a mission statement? Priority number one: heal Pembrook of its sadness. Where to next?"

"Think we need a little town flavor," Kenton said. "We're going to pay a visit to my friend, Old John. Then I think we'll try and track down the Bergs."

"Goodie," Susan said. "I love local flavor."

Edith finished her second complete shift at Steerbuck's Coffee Shop. She hung her apron in the closet and started toward the door.

"See you later," she said to Molly and Jane who were behind the counter, cleaning up the remnants from lunch.

"Enjoy this weather," Jane called.

Edith walked directly across the street and turned left down the empty sidewalk. At the first intersection, she went right and passed the post office and the Food Lion in short order. Edith loved Pembrook. She was shy by nature, and the small, sleepy town was ideal for her. Her hometown of Little Falls, Minnesota was not much different. In fact, they seemed almost like twins – separated at birth.

Edith found the thin path that led down from Broad Street to the creek that ran through town. At some point in the school year, she had selected this as her place for reflection. She sat on the creek bed's soft, warm dirt and thought about her life and the strange sense she'd always carried that her path was somehow skewed – like she'd missed a turn and mistakenly entered onto a path that looked like the right one, the real one, but was just a little bit off. She'd always felt just a little bit off.

Milo Lewis had been head of programming at CBS for a little over a year. In that time, the network had risen to number one in the rankings; Milo's black hair had gone completely gray; and his size thirty-six waist had slimmed to a size thirty-two. Nerves. Monday afternoon he entered his plush Manhattan office and sat down wearily at his desk.

This was the time of year when things got tricky. The regular season was at least somewhat obvious in terms of the shows you ran with – the ones you knew were your workhorses. It all went blurry come late May, though. This was when Milo earned his considerable salary – coming up with the replacement programming that would get them through the summer. He had a knack for staying ahead of the curve in terms of what viewers wanted to see. At least that had been the case the year before, just after he'd been promoted into this job.

He glanced through his email and clicked on a message from his old friend, Susan Clawson. They'd dated one summer many years ago and remained in contact ever since. He opened the attachment and watched a grainy music video featuring a town he didn't know and a song he'd never heard.

He sat riveted.

What is this?

Who the hell is singing?

What is Ghost Tree?

As soon as it ended, he played it again.

Things were slow. After Edith left, Molly and Jane organized everything – the closets, the cupboards, the counters, the "Fixin's Stand"; then Molly performed a monologue – Viola from *Twelfth Night*.

"That was awesome," Jane said, as they sat at the table closest to the counter, each of them falling into a relaxation stance. "Is that what you want to do with your life?"

"Pretty much," Molly replied.

"Why Harrison then? It's not exactly known for its drama department, is it?"

"Surprisingly, it's not that bad. And I didn't catch the acting bug 'til after I got here. I'll probably just head to New York after I graduate. Or maybe I'll start in Pittsburgh."

Before Jane could respond, the front door opened and a man came in, a man Jane didn't recognize at first. Sunlight framed him from behind, reminding Jane of the 1970s taciturn-cowboy version of Clint Eastwood.

"Jesus Christ," Jane whispered, standing. "I need to go talk to this guy."

"Can I come too," Molly joked – but Jane was already on the move.

"Nathan," she said as she met him by the door. "Nathan Booth? Is that really you?"

"In the flesh."

Mike was right. Nathan hadn't aged a day, and it was a little unsettling.

"Have a seat," she said.

"Actually, I was wondering if you'd be up for taking a drive. Been a little cooped up. I could use some scenery."

"Molly – I need to take off for a while. Think you can hold down the fort? Chuck will be in by three. He's never late. He's kind of creepy that way."

"No problem," Molly said. "Go have fun."

Fun? Jane wasn't sure she could do that. Now if Molly had said something like, "Go feel painfully self-conscious as you drive be-side a guy you still react to as if he's a teen heartthrob and you're the world's most heartthrob-susceptible teenaged girl," Jane could have easily said okay.

"Let's do it," Jane said to Nathan, instantly regretting her phras-ing. They left the shop and Nathan led her to his blue and white pickup truck.

"Didn't this used to be your dad's?"

"Yeah. It was just sitting out at the neighbor's house. I showed up there and Mrs. White just came out and handed me the key. Still drives okay."

"Sorry about your mom and dad," Jane said as she lifted herself into the passenger side. Nathan's parents had died of cancer within six months of one another, a dozen years before. Nathan's absence from their funerals had made some small waves locally – specula-tion, mostly, about where he was.

"You wondering why I didn't make it home back then?" he asked as he eased into drive. "I didn't know. We never talked. No one knew where I was. It wasn't until a couple years after when I needed a copy of my birth certificate. I called home and found out there wasn't one any more. I tracked down Mrs. White, and she filled me in on my orphan state."

Jane wanted to ask why it had come to that – why he'd become estranged from his roots that way. Before she could, though, she remembered that she wasn't much different. Her parents were liv-ing, still, but felt like strangers, spending their retirement down in Florida.

"Sorry, Nathan. That's pretty awful."

"It's okay. Must have been the way I wanted it. Them, too."

Moments later they were out in the country – an easy place to get to when you lived in Pembrook. Jane never tired of the rural setting. Some people needed big cities for cultural stimulation; she wasn't one of them.

They gave each other thumbnail sketches of their lives since high school. Even as he drove, it felt to Jane that Nathan could see into her soul when she spoke. He always had that effect on her. He oozed intensity – real or imagined.

"I heard about Chet," he said. "Mike came out and told me."

"Yeah. We were all pretty stunned."

They passed the field with the famous lone tree at its center. "There's the Ghost Tree," she said. When Jane was younger the sight of it would leave her spooked, but now she found it comforting. She couldn't say why.

"One night in high school I slept under it."

"You what?"

"I drove out on a Saturday night, laid out my sleeping bag and went to sleep. I was curious about the dreams I'd have."

"And?" Jane asked.

"I saw my grandmother. She died when I was little. I always had the sense that she took my family's happiness with her. She was so bright and free and fun and wild, and everyone else was pretty miserable. She brought out the little bit of good stuff in the whole brood. Then she died and the sadness took over. She was the only one fighting it. When she left, it won."

"Did she say anything to you in your dream?"

"No," Nathan said. "She just smiled at me. I felt like she was telling me it was okay to be happy. Not sure I listened. At least not then."

He turned at the burned-down Pentecostal church that had been abandoned for as long as anyone could remember. Jane knew where they were going now – Sandy Lake. She felt a flutter of excitement as if they were on a date, destined to make out like crazy in an uncomfortable back seat. Of course, the pick-up truck didn't have much of a back seat. They'd just have to make out in the front seat.

"Maybe Chet's there now," Nathan said, still referring to the Ghost Tree.

"I really can't believe he's gone," Jane confessed. "I mean – I understand that it's a fact. He's dead. And yet, my idea of this place, this town, hasn't adjusted. He's still in it."

"I don't think that needs to change," he offered. "Ever."

What was it about this boy ... this man? Jane studied his profile and considered the fact that she really didn't know Nathan Booth. Sure, she knew he had awesome hair and some kind of freak-show charisma. She knew he could sing in a way no one else she'd ever known could. She knew there was a period that summer in which they could have become something more than just band mates and that the mere sight of him still made her a little wobbly in the knees. She knew those things, yet didn't know him. Though they'd spent a whole summer standing beside one another making music, this was the most they'd ever talked. He was, for her, a mystery. Did anyone know him, she wondered – a girl ... a best friend somewhere? It was hard to imagine. Today, like twenty years ago, Nathan Booth was an island unto himself.

Mike Collins stood by Chet Howard's grave. The week's first clouds had rolled in and the day, which had been sunny, looked like rain.

Pillars of dust.

The words echoed back from his morning homily, and he pictured Chet's casket being lowered into the ground, imagined the shovelfuls of dirt being poured onto it. He understood in a new, deeper way, that our days here really are numbered.

Mike looked up as rain began to fall and wondered if his pillar of dust was the faith upon which he'd built his adult life.

"I'm lost here, God," he prayed. "Why are you leaving me stranded? Why would you lead me so far, just to leave me alone?"

For a few moments longer he let himself soak. He wiped his eyes and walked back to his car.

They tried the Smoke Shop first. Old John was pretty much a fixture there. They'd missed his morning chess match, though, and were directed to Jane's where the old man liked to drink his afternoon decaf. They found him stationed at the café counter. He was the lone afternoon customer.

Kenton was excited to realize that the barista talking with Old John was none other than Molly Faber, the recipient of Chet Howard's dying wish. "That's the girl I saw talking with Father Mike," he whispered to Susan. "Molly."

"Cool."

"Hey, Old John," Kenton said as they reached the counter. "How's it going?"

"Quite well, my boy. Quite well."

Kenton, like most Pembrook natives, loved Old John. It seemed that each resident had a different story, a different memorable Old John conversation. Kenton's appreciation had grown roots when, as a high school student, he had spent most afternoons playing chess with John in lieu of the sports and plays in which most other kids were engaged.

"I heard a rumor you were back in town," John said.

"Yeah," Kenton said. "We're doing a documentary about Pembrook. I wondered if we could talk to you a little, on camera. You know – interview you."

"Interview me? You must be delirious, child. I'm about as boring as they come."

"Well, would you mind being boring on camera?" Susan asked. Kenton was grateful she'd chosen then to step in. Everyone knew that Old John was unable to resist a woman's smile, and Susan's was pretty much as potent as they came.

"For you, I suppose," John said. "Just don't expect too much."

Susan's cell phone rang, and she stepped away to answer it. Mandy, meanwhile, set about creating a studio of sorts, toward the front of the room where the light was the strongest. John and Kenton took seats at the table she clearly intended as home base. Kenton made small talk, happy to notice that Susan had ended her call and was talking with Molly, who was nodding and smiling the way everyone seemed to when they talked with Susan Clawson.

Old John was everything Kenton hoped he'd be. Though he didn't have much to say about the band, he did remember them and recalled the brief sensation they caused that summer long ago. His greatest value came from the town history he provided.

"Pembrook was actually a coal town in the late 1800s," Old John explained, talking to the camera as if he'd been doing it for years. "About seven miles east of here there were mines. Thriving mines from what I understand. A Scotsman named Thornton Pembrook owned the land and ran the whole operation, and that's how the town got its name, obviously. Unbeknownst to anybody, though, the mines were relatively shallow. So, as Pittsburgh and Youngstown and places like that continued to produce mass quantities of coal, Pembrook kind of fell off the map, so to speak. Thornton eventually moved back to Scotland, and most of the laborers moved to those other towns I mentioned. A few brave souls remained, and they are the humble folks we descended from."

Old John also provided the local lore about the Ghost Tree after which the band had been named. All in all, he was documentary pay dirt, and Kenton was thrilled with the results.

Molly followed. Susan took Kenton's place at the interview table, and Kenton watched as the former beauty queen made Molly feel totally at ease, as if they were old friends shooting the breeze over some coffee. Soon the confident co-ed was pouring out the story of her brief friendship with Chet Howard. Mandy and Kenton exchanged knowing nods as the interview hit its crux, the moment when Chet spoke the fateful words through his coma fog, words that ultimately led them all there: *"Ghost Tree. Reunite the band."*

Again. Pay dirt.

A half hour later as the trio lugged their gear from the suddenly bustling coffee shop (word had spread of the "big Hollywood movie" being shot at Jane's) and out into the rainy late afternoon, Susan dropped her bombshell.

"That was a friend of mine from CBS." She motioned to her phone. "He wants to put Ghost Tree on national TV."

The rain fell hard. Jane and Nathan sat watching as the army of drops attacked the surface of the lake.

"Chet said something about reuniting the band," Jane said. "Just before he died he mentioned Ghost Tree playing again."

Nathan said nothing. The sight of the rain on the water had him hypnotized. His mind drifted to that summer. He remembered the power he had felt when the five of them played together – every single time, without fail. Even when some of the rehearsals seemed fruitless, he was still high afterwards.

"Did you hear me, Nathan?"

"Yeah. I was just remembering."

"Remembering what?"

The rain softened suddenly – going from a beating to a pattering on the car hood and windshield.

"Playing with you guys. That was just about the best feeling I ever had."

"Me, too."

"The rest of my life sucked pretty bad, Jane. My dad was tough. Really tough. Playing with you guys was my only peace."

Nathan turned quiet. Jane frowned against the soft blanket of gray late-day sky.

"Ancient history," he added.

"Sometimes it doesn't feel that way."

He waited for her to say more. When she didn't, he started the truck and backed away from the lake.

"Milo who?"

Susan couldn't help smiling at Kenton. He was so completely oblivious to aspects of reality that consumed most others; aspects such as appearance and wealth. He was a man focused on one thing: bringing visions to life, whatever those visions might be. She was sure he was clueless about her attraction to him, which, of course, made her all the more attracted. Funny how that worked.

"Milo Lewis," she said. "He works for CBS."

"What's he do?" Kenton said, in obvious need of clarification.

"Something with programming. I think he has juice. We dated a few times, many moons ago."

"And all he saw was the video from last night?"

She nodded. "I emailed it to him just before I went to sleep last night."

"What does he think it is?"

"He's not sure. He asked me the same thing. He was just curious, and the more I talked, the more curious he became."

"This is starting to feel a little weird," Kenton said.

"I think this is how all good things are supposed to feel. Don't over-analyze."

"Amen," Mandy called from the back seat, smiling like the world's happiest bulldog.

"So how'd you leave it?" Kenton asked.

"I told him we'd send him more over the next couple of days, and keep talking. He may eventually want to send a bigger crew here, but for now he seems content to let us do our thing."

"Is that what we even want?" Kenton wondered. "A big major-network thing?"

"It would be big bucks, Kenton," Susan said. "Not that that matters too much. It would also probably be the biggest audience Ghost Tree could ever hope to reach in a million years."

The rain stopped by the time they made it to the Bergs' private dirt road. The sun was making a late-day rally – and seemed on the brink of winning the game, against all odds.

"It feels so clean out here," Susan said, inhaling the country air as deeply as her lungs would allow once they'd emerged from the car. "I'm sure it always feels this way, but the rain just kind of heightens it or something. I feel like I'm breathing in pure oxygen."

Mandy grabbed her gear from the trunk, saying something about a television show she shot once in Denver, Colorado. Kenton went ahead to the Bergs' front door. Ron Berg emerged before Kenton made it there, smiling and opening his arms in welcome.

"Well, hello," he said. "What's this I hear about a movie being made in our little town?"

Ron's wife, Lisa, appeared at the door and called hello. She was short and petite with brown hair down to her shoulders.

"Hey," Ron said, "before we go to the place where they rehearsed, I wanted to show you something."

"I'm Susan," Susan said as she reached them on the porch. Mandy followed close behind. "This is our camera wiz, Mandy."

The Bergs greeted both women and ushered the group through the kitchen and on into the living room.

"Have a seat, have a seat," Ron said in a voice that reminded Susan of a show she remembered vaguely from childhood – H.R. *Pufnstuf*; Ron sounded like one of Witchie Poo's cronies. "After you called, I dug around in the basement and I found this." He lifted an empty videotape box from the top of the television. "I had a feeling I recorded one of Ghost Tree's rehearsals way back when, but had no idea where it was. Luckily, I found it!"

"Things have kind of been going that way," Susan noted. "Right, Kenton?" She was aware of the excitement in the room as she took a seat on the comfortable old sofa the Bergs had clearly put to good use. Kenton sat beside her and Mandy stood to the side, capturing the moments, as always.

Lisa handed each of them a can of Budweiser, and they watched as Ron pressed a button and the screen lit up with the interior of the barn. The band members formed an imperfect circle, more of an oval really, with Nathan and Jane flanking the sliding doors and Kenny Maxim's kit centered against the giant old fire truck that stood parallel with the barn's rear wall. Clearly, they were not affected by the presence of the video recorder.

"Did they know they were being recorded?" Susan asked.

"I don't know," Ron said. "It seems to me that they didn't. I really don't remember though. This is so strange. I can't believe I still had this."

Susan had seen footage of "visionaries" in Medjugorje being visited by the Virgin Mary and, in a strange way, that's what the scene
on the television reminded her of. For the first few minutes there
was small talk and tinkering with knobs and instruments, but then
it was like they all fell into a trance. No one spoke. It was as if they
were all seeing something that was visible only to them.

During the first portion, as the band mates were seeking some
common musical terrain, and it all sounded more or less like nonsense, Ron Berg confessed that he never quite "got" Ghost Tree.

"I mean I really liked them all as people," he said. "The music,
though, I didn't get it. I couldn't hear it. I'm more of a traditional
rhythm and blues guy, I guess."

"Oh, I could," his wife said. "Most nights when Kenton was
spying through the side window, I was sitting right beside him. I
couldn't get enough of it."

At that moment, Nathan Booth's voice could be heard emerg-
ing through what had become a more patterned chord progression.
It was as if he was chanting, but gradually more and more words
could be discerned, along with an actual melody. His eyes were
closed and his lips touched the microphone as he sang.

It seemed to Susan that the listeners leaned forward collectively
as the song shifted into what she supposed would be called the
chorus – though they inhabited it for a good three minutes, Nathan
voice-fishing and the rest of the band seeking out spaces above and
below, beside and behind.

"Can we borrow this, Ron?" she asked.

"Of course," he said eagerly. "I was hoping you would. Now let
me show you that barn."

Wednesday evening, Father Mike, who had been criminally neg-
ligent in his priestly duties of late, was trying to reinsert his head
into the faith game. This was the night each week earmarked for
homily preparation, and that was what he planned to do. He'd gone

further than expected with the "pillars of dust" idea and felt it was no longer useable – homilist's code of ethics.

Armed with a steaming cup of Earl Gray tea and a bowl of Chips Ahoy chocolate chip cookies he retreated to his office and settled in behind his cluttered rosewood desk. The gospel for Sunday was a letter from Saint Paul, encouraging Thessalonians to join the body of Christ. By the light of a pair of tall candles, Mike sat reflecting on his own place within that body, and began to type.

"It's raining again." Jane sang the old Supertramp song off-key in the doorway. "Crazy weather day, eh?"

"Jesus, Jane," Mike said. "You scared the hell out of me."

"You're not supposed to say 'Jesus' like that are you?" She un-zipped her navy blue hooded sweatshirt, wet with the day's second round of rainfall, and walked into the room. "So this is where all the deep, priestly shit springs forth, huh?"

"You've been in my office before," Mike said. "You helped me move in."

"It wasn't your office then. It was just a room with boxes. Now it's your special place. I can feel it. I'm having an odd urge to confess my sins."

Mike was thankful for the dim lighting, suddenly embarrassed by the posters of country roads and wall signs bearing simplistic slogans of encouragement. That kind of stuff made Jane nauseous.

"You'll never guess who I just took a drive through the country with," Jane said.

"Nathan?"

"He surprised me at the shop this afternoon." She took a seat at one of the two red-cushioned chairs that sat on the wisdom-receiv-ing side of the desk. "You were right by the way. He hasn't aged a day. Freaked me out. I felt so old and ugly – and yet like a high school girl at the same time."

Mike felt like he was in high school, too. The inside of him ached like it had back then – with some sharp-edged need he couldn't name. He looked away. Jane reached across the desk and grabbed a cookie from the bowl.

"You haven't really aged either, Jane," he said, looking back at her. "Don't let it go to your head."

"You're a priest. You're supposed to say kind things."

At that moment, Mike wished he wasn't a priest. He wished Jane could see him for the man he was, the way she saw Nathan.

"How did it go? What did you guys talk about?"

"We really didn't talk much," she said. "We just kind of drove. And then we kind of sat by the lake. We had wild, animalistic sex, and then he brought me straight back to the shop."

"Cool," Mike said. "Did you tell him about Chet?"

"Yeah. He said that playing with us was the best thing he ever did – or something like that. I think he'd do a show if we all were up for it." Neither one of them said anything. The rain grew louder against the window. "Are we? What are you thinking? A Ghost Tree reunion?"

Mike suddenly felt the rush of possibility – not regarding the band, but about baring his soul to his best friend, the woman he still loved. He could almost taste the words he would use to tell her everything – almost hear them joining them in the room right then like lost children, clamoring for love and affection. Instead of disclosing his own secrets, though, he invited Jane to share hers.

"Did you talk about anything else?"

Jane seemed to look everywhere except at Mike. Finally she met his eyes with hers. He couldn't be sure, but they seemed to be shining with moisture.

"Not really."

"Are you okay, Jane?"

"Not really," she said again.

She gripped the arms of her chair and seemed to will herself back to composure.

"You want to talk about it?"

"Not really," she repeated for the third time. "Thinking about the band is bringing up some old stuff. Stuff I probably should have dealt with a long time ago. I'll sort through it."

He almost said something about the fact that she'd had twenty years and what the hell was she waiting for, but opted for "Well if you need any help, I'm here for you" instead, sounding like good old Mike the priest again.

"Understood."

Her tone indicated that the emotional portion of the conversation had concluded.

"I went to the Landmark last night," Mike said.

"Has Father Michael taken to the bottle then?" she asked in a brogue that easily rivaled Mike's for its utter and complete lameness.

He proceeded to give her a synopsis of his drunken night, which segued into the visit he'd received that morning from Kenton.

"Are you freaking kidding me? Kenton wants to make a movie about Ghost Tree?"

"I think he already is," Mike said. "I'm sure they'll be tracking you down soon."

"Jesus, Mike! It feels like there's some cosmic conspiracy going on. Don't you think there's some strange shit going down here?"

Mike knew there was no real need to answer. But still he did – in his best melodramatic Horatio from CSI Miami. Pretending to push his imaginary sunglasses back up the bridge of his nose, he said, "That, my friend," long pause, "is the million dollar question." Then broke into the opening of the Who song.

Jane laughed.

An hour later, with Jane gone and his homily abandoned, Mike sat on his bed digging through the box he'd dragged from the back of his closet. Before long he located one of the cassettes marked GT and put it into his ancient little stereo alarm clock.

Anytime the band felt like they'd gotten something to a place where it could rightfully be called a song, he'd set up room microphones and record. Through the hiss he heard the voice of Kenny Maxim counting them off. A song called *She Took the Key* came on.

It was a driving, carefree, reckless rocker, and Mike remembered that it had always been one of his favorites – a little simpler and more direct than their other creations.

"Damn," he thought. "We were good."

Closing his eyes, he was transported to that summer, those nights, with four kindred spirits. It really was magic. And each time they made music Mike was consciously aware – in the way only an eighteen-year old can be – of its importance, and of the fact that it, the music, superseded his ego, and his jealousy, and even his unrequited love. Would it feel that way still, he wondered? Would playing songs with Ghost Tree still hold that cleansing power, that instant perspective? Would a band reunion mean Jane finally would have to come clean about her mysterious decision to skip town?

In that moment, with the night growing late and the hard rain subsiding again, he decided that he had no choice, really. He needed to find out. And would.

Nathan dreamed of vast, barren desert. Barefoot, he walked, and then flew, weightless above the waved, golden sand. He landed on a mountain cliff and stood even with the sky, which cracked, revealing a changing kaleidoscope of faces: his father's, his mother's, his grandmother's, Chet Howard's, Jane Taylor's, Mike Collins' and finally, his. The standing-on-the-cliff Nathan smiled beneficently at his stoic, expressionless mirror image.

"I am love."

"I am light."

"I am joy."

He murmured these words to himself in his sleep.

4

Jonathon Hilliard was always the first to arrive at the Admissions Building – which was the first building you came to when you entered the campus of Harrison College. Thursday morning, though, he was surprised to find a trio of bleary-eyed visitors (one of whom seemed to be operating a hand-held camera) awaiting him outside the front door.

"Hi, Kenton," Jonathon said before being introduced to the bespectacled filmmaker's female companions. "I saw that Ghost Tree video on YouTube." The cheerful dean took quiet satisfaction in his use of the hip terminology. "Nice stuff."

"She gets most of the credit," Susan chimed, aiming an elbow at Mandy who stopped recording long enough to take a small bow. "She's Mandy. I'm Susan."

"Nice to meet you both. But I have to tell you I'm a little confused about what you're doing. Why would you or anyone else care about Ghost Tree?"

Susan supplied the story of Chet's deathbed directive, and Kenton explained that they weren't entirely sure what they were doing, but that they were hoping Ghost Tree might actually reunite for a show.

"Are you kidding me?" Jonathon's pink cheeks grew pinker, contrasting with his short, dark red hair. "You want us to play again?"

"That's the plan," said Susan.

"Any chance we could go into your office and get an interview?" Kenton asked.

Ten minutes later, after Mandy had a chance to gauge the lighting from the giant window, set up a camera to supplement her hand-held, and place a small microphone on the wiry Dean's jacket lapel, they were ready. Jonathon sat behind his desk but at a slight angle as Mandy had requested. Kenton and Susan sat across from him.

"So tell us who you are and what you played," Susan said.

"My name is Jonathon Hilliard, and I was the keyboard player for Ghost Tree," he said, unsure of where to direct his words, wavering between his interviewers, the camera, and his clasped hands.

"Just talk to us directly, Jonathon," Susan said. "Try and forget the cameras are even here. Now tell us again who you are."

"My name is Jonathon Hilliard. I played piano and organ in Ghost Tree."

"Who came up with the band name?" Kenton asked.

"I think that was Nathan."

"When was the last time you saw Nathan?"

This question was posed by Mandy in a tone that suggested that the answer he gave would be the place she visited next.

"The last time I saw Nathan was the last time we played together. It was a local festival called Strawberry Days. You know what I'm talking about, Kenton. It happens every year in August."

"Was it a good gig?" Kenton asked.

"It was an excellent gig. I mean really excellent. We were getting better and better, and I remember feeling like the sky was the limit. People were eating it up."

"Then what happened?" asked Susan. "I mean after that show. Why was that the end?"

"To this day I don't have the answer to that question," he said. "I was never really sure who left first, Jane or Nathan. They were both just suddenly gone. A month later, I started college here. Mike went to college in Erie. Ghost Tree just died."

His strained laugh indicated that he didn't find it particularly amusing.

"Did you ever ask anyone about it?" Kenton said.

"Well, Chet was as clueless as I was. Kenny was too. Mike didn't really want to talk about it. And by the time Jane got back, Nathan had fallen off the grid, so it didn't seem like it mattered too much anyway." He paused. Thinking. Lifting his shoulders up and down. "It's a total mystery. One minute we were flying high and the next it was like we had never played a note together. Of course, over time, I stopped caring so much about it. But for a while it drove me crazy."

"Were you angry?" Susan asked.

"Yeah," he said. "I was. But I was more confused than anything. We all seemed so committed."

"If all the other members of the band agreed to play another show, would you do it?" asked Susan.

"Good luck finding Nathan," he said.

"Actually – he's back in Pembrook," Kenton said, "or near Pembrook. He lives in a cabin not far from here."

"Well, I'll be darned," Jonathon said. "Yeah, I'd play. Why not?"

He was onto something. He knew it. Milo Lewis had a sixth sense that way. If there had been any doubt before, the second wave of footage Susan sent wiped it away. Ghost Tree was golden. He could feel it in his bones.

A different song accompanied batch two – some of which matched the footage of the band rehearsing. Susan also sent some great sound bites courtesy of an old man who'd lived in the town forever, and the couple whose barn housed the band's rehearsals. The kicker, though, was the college student who explained about the band-manager's dying request.

"Ghost Tree – reunite the band."

Milo hung on her every syllable. No actor could have said the words better.

"Programming gold," he thought. "I can feel it in my bones."

Edith squirted whipped cream onto the top of the White Mocha she'd been preparing, then handed it over the counter to Mrs. Moreland.

"Thank you, dear," the retired grade school music teacher said. "My last guilty pleasure." She lifted the frothy beverage to her lips.

"You're welcome, Mrs. Moreland." Edith watched as the gray-haired woman joined her two friends at a table. "I need a quick bathroom break, Molly."

The work schedule throughout the week had been that Edith opened each day with Jane, then Molly showed up mid-morning and worked until a few hours after Edith was done.

"Go," Molly said.

In the spacious and comfortable unisex bathroom at the rear of the shop, Edith turned on the light and stood at the sink. She studied her face in the mirror. Thin, brown hair fell across her horn-rimmed glasses. Her complexion was pale and clear, her eyes, coal-gray, bright, happy.

Ever since she was a little girl, Edith had what her mother called "bad nerves." She used to gnaw through the cuffs and collars on her shirts and always had a chewed-up mitten in her mouth during the cold Minnesota winters. She was needlessly nervous all the time and was always the last kid to try things like riding a bike, jumping in the pool, or telling a joke. Early adolescence was a little better, but later into her teenage years the anxiety reasserted itself. She spent much of her time in high school hidden in the girls' bathroom, crying.

At fifteen, she had her first real panic attack – one that put her in the Emergency Room. She hyperventilated so badly that all the muscles in her body contracted, and she couldn't move. Her father had to carry her into the hospital where they gave her a mask to control her breathing and shot her up with Ativan. She remembered the doctor telling her terrified parents, "This is not normal. Your daughter needs help."

And she got it. She went to behavioral therapy and saw a psychiatrist. After almost three years she found some semblance of normalcy, thanks to the coping techniques she'd learned and the particular medication they'd finally deduced was the right one for her. She welcomed the normalcy, of course, but didn't like the disconnected, lethargic way the pills sometimes made her feel.

She nodded with a smile and thought, "I'm better now. I know I am."

Edith reached into her pocket and pulled out a small plastic bag containing a single, tiny pill. Without hesitating or giving herself a chance for second-guessing, she threw the white Lexapro capsule into the toilet and flushed it down.

"Wow, Mike – you really did a one-eighty, man. Yesterday morning I wasn't even sure if you'd let us talk to you again."

"I had a dark night of the soul."

Kenton was glad Mike was dressed in his priestly blacks. He liked the contrast between priest-in-black-Mike and twenty-years-ago-jeans-and-T-shirt-Mike. And Kenton was thrilled to receive the CD Mike had just handed over containing rehearsal versions of the nine Ghost Tree originals.

"Ghost Tree has just been upgraded from a tropical storm to a class four hurricane," Susan whispered to Kenton as Mike led them to the rectory's living room, which was more like a regular house's living room, replete with quilts and coffee stains, than Kenton would have expected. As Mandy set up the camera, Kenton asked if it was okay to play the disc, and Mike nodded.

"What's this one called?" Susan asked as the first song began.

"*She Took the Key.*"

Susan started moving to it with a degree of unselfconsciousness Kenton could only dream about. Though he thought he'd moved admirably past his piercing awareness that Susan Clawson was, as far as he could tell, perfect in all ways, he wasn't so sure any more.

His connection with her was beginning to fuel his optimism as much as their run of good luck was.

"I remember this song," Kenton said. "It was always my favorite."

"Mine, too," Mike agreed.

"I'm still stuck on *Mystic Light*," Mandy said. "I want that song played at my funeral."

She clipped a microphone to the priest's shirt and asked him to sit in the chair that was closest to the window. Susan turned down the music slightly and joined Kenton on the sofa. Mandy roamed.

They went through the standard string of getting-acquainted questions, then Susan dug deeper. She led Mike down a path of memories, recounting the gigs, the rehearsals, and the roles they'd all played.

"So why did the band disintegrate?" Susan asked finally. "It sounds like you guys were just about to take flight, and then people started disappearing."

"It's a little hard to remember now," Mike said. "I think I kind of minimized everything to have it make more sense, or something."

Susan nodded. Kenton loved the way that Susan nodded.

"I forced it into a cliché. I was one of a million kids who played in a rock band that played a few gigs and never went anywhere."

"But?"

"But I knew there was something special about what we did." He paused. "The reason we disintegrated, I think, is that we were all at that age when you make your big decisions, you know? As you graduate high school you decide if you'll go to college. If you decide to go to college, you need to choose which one. We'd all made those types of choices before the band played a note … so a few key turns led us all back to our pre-appointed paths. You can really just chalk it up to bad timing."

"So, Mike," Susan said next, surprising Kenton by not applying some more verbal scrutiny to what the squirming priest had just said, "would you honor your old manager's last request and play one more show with Ghost Tree?"

"Yes, I would," Mike said with more conviction than Kenton could ever have predicted.

"I'm not buying the whole bad-timing thing," Kenton said once they were tucked safely back in his ancient Volvo and had driven a few miles from Saint Luke's. "I'm surprised you let that one go."

"All in good time, my dear Watson," Susan said. "But I agree that for a priest, he's not a very good liar. There is definitely more to that story. Eventually we'll find out who made which wrong turns. That's a promise. Where exactly are you taking us, Mister Hall?"

Kenton was pulling into a place called 'The Landmark Bar and Hotel,' according to the dilapidated road sign out front. They were in search of more local flavor, Susan supposed. She loved it instantly – all worn down and ragged and rising from a sea of brown dirt and black gravel.

"This is my kind of place, dude."

"Thought you might like it. Don't expect too much as far as the food goes, though."

They went inside to find only one paying customer at this early hour – a slight man with a pale, mustached face, sitting on the middle stool. He wore a red St. Louis Cardinal's hat and a stoic expression.

"Hey, Larry," Kenton said.

Susan was amazed at the way Kenton the shy guy was on a first-name basis with every single resident of the town. Only Lou from the Cloverleaf fell beyond the filmmaker's impressive reach.

"Hey, Movie Man," Larry called. "What're you drinking?"

"Bud and Jack," Susan said, sensing she'd found their next interview. She took the stool right next to the solitary drinker.

"A woman after my own heart." Larry said. "Bud and Jack for the lady and me, Pete."

The bartender, who stood only slightly taller than five feet and had the same number of teeth as he had fingers, snatched a ten from Larry's money pile and set Susan up.

"Why thank you," she said. The instant Pete set the shot down she drank it, wanting to win Larry's trust.

"One more," Larry said.

"Yeah, one more," Susan echoed.

"I'll have a diet coke," Kenton said.

"Same here," said Mandy.

"So are you guys gonna make me a movie star or what?"

"Something like that," Susan said.

"She's getting my bad side, by the way," Larry said, referring to Mandy, who was standing to his right with the camera raised and running.

"Actually, Larry, we're doing a documentary about Ghost Tree," Kenton explained.

"Ghost Tree?"

"Not the actual tree," Kenton clarified. "A band that was together here about twenty years ago … you remember them at all? Mike Collins played bass. Jane Taylor played guitar. Nathan Booth was the lead singer."

"I saw Mike the other night," Larry said. "He was here tying one on. Sat right beside me. I thought it was a little strange, him being a priest and all. He was even singing along to *Sympathy For the Devil.*" The professional drinker employed his craft, downing the whiskey and half a beer in a matter of seconds. "But I don't judge. I'm sure he had his reasons."

"Do you remember the band?" Susan asked.

It was just a different kind of person you met in a small town, she thought. Characters like Larry and Old John were hard to come by in Manhattan or the West Village. Or maybe they were there, but everyone was in too big of a hurry to stop and talk to them.

"As a matter of fact I do," Larry said, smiling as if he was learning of his own knowledge in the same moment that they were. "I remember them really well."

"Tell us, Larry." Susan followed her second shot with a healthy sip of beer. She hadn't had a buzz like this in years. It felt good.

"I actually never saw the band. But I used to work the three-toeleven shift at the Wendell August Forge, and would walk home past Berg's Farm every night. I've never owned a car. Don't believe in 'em."

"I'm with you, " Susan said. "I don't have a car either."

She failed to mention that the majority of New Yorkers lived car-less.

"Most nights I'd hear the music from the road when I walked home. So I can't give you any real scoop on what they sounded like. Sounded good from a distance, though. But I can tell you about one night that summer. I finished my shift, and passed Berg's about ten minutes after that. I heard somebody crying in the woods right by the road there. You know how there's that dirt path that leads up to the farm – Berg Lane, I think they call it?" He directed this question to Kenton, who nodded. "Well there's woods on both sides of it, and that's where the girl was."

"Did you stop to check on the her?"

"Well of course, I did. I hear a lady crying I'm gonna stop to help. It's just my way."

"So what happened?" Susan asked. "Did she tell you what was wrong? It was Jane Taylor, right?"

"Yeah, it was Janie," Larry replied. "When I asked her if she need-ed any help, she waved me off. Told her I'd walk her home, but she pointed to her bike, said she'd be okay. To be honest, I could tell she just wanted me to leave her the hell alone, so I did."

"Interesting," Susan said. "Do you remember when this was in the summer, Larry?"

"No. I just know it was summer. I only had that job for a couple of months."

"Next round's on me," Susan declared, as Pete eagerly brought them replacements.

He always spent Thursday afternoons at the hospital – visiting with patients and distributing communion to those who wanted it. Father Mike drove there as scheduled but kept driving, past the hospital entrance, past the ramp down to the interstate. On and on he drove. All the while, he listened to the CD he'd dubbed for himself of the nine Ghost Tree songs – nine songs from a lifetime ago. As he listened, the scenes played in his head.

Their seven gigs: the first one, a party at the public pool, with all of them trembling and nervous and loving every minute; the second, a private event at the Sportsman's Club – for a high school kid's birthday; the third, fourth, and fifth, three consecutive Saturdays in July at 'Gregory's Commons,' a bar ten miles away from town with a bigger crowd each week; the sixth, an August show in Pittsburgh – one of six bands in a dive bar a block away from Carnegie Mellon University; and, finally, Strawberry Days.

Seven shows and Mike remembered each one like it was yesterday. He remembered Jane grooving and smiling, reflecting off light. He remembered Nathan commanding each audience without even knowing he was doing it. He remembered Jonathon smiling like a maniac, completely lost to the music. He remembered Kenny leading them forward with his strong, steady kick drum, driving the proceedings as Mike and his bass held on for dear life. He remembered the sweat, the smell of the microphones, the faces of the sound engineers, and the audience members, the load-ins, the stages, the songs. He remembered it all.

He also remembered the Monday morning after Strawberry Days when Jane showed up at his house, announced she was leaving, and asked Mike to pass along the news to the band. She'd been in a funk but had seemed to shake it off at the gig.

"I'm going to Pittsburgh," she'd said with resignation in her voice. "My dad wants me to go to Pitt like I'd planned. He doesn't give a rat's ass about the band."

In previous weeks the band members had made a hobby of talking through the ways they each could alter their plans for the fall, each one more than willing to delay their big life-moves in favor of exploring where the band might take them. Jane had spoken a bit less adamantly than the others but, still, seemed to be with the program.

Mike hoped it would be the opportunity she needed to stand up to her bastard of a father. It hadn't been. By the time Mike saw her again, almost a year had passed. The band was fading into memory, and Mike was already in college and on the winding road to priesthood.

Mike wondered to himself if he hadn't been secretly relieved at his best friend's abrupt departure. The pain of carrying around his true feelings for her, unspoken and gaining mass with each passing day, had grown tiresome, not to mention nearly impossible. He'd felt as if he might explode with the tension. Was that the reason he hadn't said anything to her? He could have come clean with her that morning. She'd paused, he remembered, leaving an opening for him to say something.

And yet he hadn't.

"I need to run some errands, Martha."

Jonathon Hilliard uttered this statement, a bold-faced lie, into the base of his office phone. His secretary, he knew, would accept it for truth. The pitfalls of power.

He left his sport coat on the back of his chair and headed out into the welcoming afternoon sunlight. He walked at a good clip up the vacant campus, past the Kessler Dormitory, the Charles Pavlick Memorial Library, the James Bedore Computer Center, and the Carol Kerr Cafeteria until reaching the Pew Fine Arts Center, which housed the newly-renovated state-of-the-art performance hall, along with several classrooms and rehearsal spaces.

He went through the glass front doors and hesitated; deciding between downstairs privacy and upstairs grandeur – he opted for the latter. The massive main room where all of the full-scale theatrical productions took place was empty, as he expected it to be. The moment he entered he spied his stately destination.

Moments later he sat down, center stage, at the grand piano, lifted the heavy black lid, and rested his fingers on the sparkling keys. He closed his eyes and waited for the chords to jump across the synapses of his cerebral cortex. Silence was replaced by rich, beautiful, glorious sound, as his hands moved before he even knew they'd started.

His voice was thin and indistinct, nothing like Nathan's, and no match for the piano. But still he sang.

> *I been searching for my mystic light*
> *Searching for my mystic light*
> *Searching for my mystic light*
> *Searching for my mystic light.*

Tears streamed from his eyes as he allowed himself to feel it returning – the power from long ago – when they'd stood on a cloud high above the world and smiled down.

Mitch Dononfeld ran the business affairs department at CBS. Milo had spoken with him Thursday morning, outlining what he wanted to have happen; he'd received a contract draft late that afternoon. With papers in hand, he called Susan's cell phone.

"Hello?"

He was thrown by the sound of her living voice. These days, it seemed no one ever answered – which was fine by Milo. Susan, of course, was an exception to everything. She was, by far, the prettiest woman he had ever dated … and, at the same time, the one requiring the least maintenance. Milo would have thought that would make her his dream woman for all eternity, but ultimately the chemistry had just not been there. It was nice to have exceptional friends, though, and Susan was certainly that – exceptional.

"Susan. I didn't expect you to answer."

"You want me to hang up on you, Milo?"

"No, no, no, of course not. How's it going out there?"

Milo had long ago learned the trick of acting like he was part of something before he had actually acquired official access. It was one of his guiding business techniques: positive visualization given wings and a voice.

"If I told you it couldn't be going any better, it would be an understatement," she said, her voice in perpetual rasp. "Every little thing is going our way. We got that rehearsal footage, old bootlegs of Ghost Tree's nine original songs. We're two for two on getting band members to commit to the reunion show. And there's a mystery to their breakup that seems to be guiding everything. It's perfect, Milo. I'm trying not to think about it. Don't want to break the spell."

"That sounds amazing, Susan. And I have to tell you, I'm pretty intrigued by the whole thing."

"Like, how intrigued?" she asked.

"Intrigued enough that I had my money people draw up some deal points," he explained. "I want you to commit to exploring whatever the hell this turns out to be through my network. Maybe it's just a four-week thing and I try to find two other stories to follow to see me through the summer. Once this one pops, I think old bands will be coming out of the woodwork to get their due. Do you think we could get four hours out of what you're doing? That translates into under three hours of actual air time."

"Yeah, Milo – I think we'll have that easily. We're just trying to figure out if it isn't a feature film."

"Who's to say it can't be both?" Milo was suddenly nervous. He wasn't used to dealing with people who weren't driven by money and ego. The thought of losing Ghost Tree was unacceptable to him. "I'm willing to offer you guys $250,000 per episode and I'll cover any extra budgeting ... if we need to send you a bigger crew ... or anything else you might need." Silence on the line. "And I'll reimburse you for all your expenses ... you know, gas and hotels and all that." Still silent. "You there, Susan?"

"Yeah, I'm here. I'm just thinking. Let me get back to you."

He gave her every possible number he could think of, wanting to obliterate the possibility of missing her call.

"Call me any time. I think we can make some magic here, Susan."

"I think we already are, Milo. Good talking to you."

Artistic types. Who could figure them?

"Holy shit!"

Susan screamed those words as she walked back inside 'The Landmark'. Kenton and Mandy were finishing off their second tray of chicken wings. Kenton couldn't determine if the former beauty queen's exclamation was voiced in joy or horror.

"Holy Shit," she said again as she took her seat at the table they'd occupied since concluding their interview of Larry Terk.

"Good holy shit or bad holy shit?" Mandy asked.

"Good, I think."

"What's up?" Kenton asked.

"That was Milo from CBS. He really wants to do something with us, guys. I mean he's ready to send us a contract right this second?"

"Jesus," Kenton said.

"Yeah – and he's throwing around some nice dollar figures."

Kenton's mind raced – first in pursuit of the momentary flutter that the thought of actually making money for his art always caused but then closer to reality and to the ramifications of what the involvement of a major television network would be. His experience with corporate gigs, which was exactly what a show on CBS would be, had not been negative, but he'd always known where he stood – on the receiving end of the orders – and accepted that before signing on. This was different, though. This was their baby. This was something they would need to let be, whatever it was. Kenton knew the moment Milo Lewis or any of the other executives at CBS got involved, they'd be unable to keep themselves from forcing their own visions and expectations onto things. That was simply the way it worked.

"What?" Susan asked. "Can you please let us into the mystery of Kenton's brain?"

"You look like you're about to faint," Mandy added. "Deep breaths, buddy."

"I just don't want anyone to fuck up what we have going here," Kenton said. The others nodded. "It all feels too good to hand over the reins even a little bit."

"So we won't," Susan said. "I'll tell Milo that the only way we'll play ball with them is if they let us see it through completely on our own unless we decide otherwise."

"Do you think he'd go for that?" Mandy asked.

"I do."

Kenton looked at his cohorts. He'd worked well with people throughout his career but couldn't remember liking any as much as he liked these two. Mandy, with her technical tenacity and fireplug physique, Susan with her overflowing spirit and her easy-going way.

"Do you think you can pull it off visually?" he asked Mandy.

"It'll look pretty much like it's been looking. But I'm liking the way it's been looking. Aren't you guys?"

Kenton and Susan nodded their agreement.

"And Milo must be too," Susan said. "All he's going on is the couple of short clips I've sent him."

"I'm in if you guys are," Kenton said.

Susan placed her hand face down in the center of the table, beside the sauce-littered wing basket.

"Let's do this," she said as Mandy placed her hand atop hers and Kenton placed his atop Mandy's. Susan then moved hers from the bottom to the top and the others did the same, climbing an invisible ladder.

"I'll let Milo squirm a little then call him back this evening."

As the team stood and walked to the door, Larry Terk called, "Let's hook up later, so we can make our own private movie." The slurred words were directed at Susan and laced with booze-addled lust. For the first time since their arrival, Kenton was embarrassed by his hometown.

Though Jane was a regular runner, her ten-speed bike had been sitting unused in the garage for over a year. She dragged it out late in the day Thursday and set off up Route 29, away from Pembrook, away from everything. She pedaled as hard and as fast as she could in an effort to manufacture enough wind in her face to blow her worries away. It didn't work. By the time she pulled off the road, the sweat soaked through her T-shirt, but her mind was as cluttered as ever.

She laid the bike on the edge of the pavement and walked into the large field. The Ghost Tree towered, alone, in the middle. Melodrama had never been Jane's style, but this seemed like a good place to sit alone and sort through her feelings.

"Okay, big ol' tree of spirits," she thought, "here I am. Let's talk."

She closed her eyes and continued aloud. She would have looked like a crazy person to a passer-by.

"First, off, I'm pissed about Chet. He died too soon, too young, too far from our last good conversation. It isn't fair."

The leaves rustled softly in reply.

"Then there's this general uneasiness I'm feeling with all the talk of a Ghost Tree reunion. It's not all negative, I suppose. I mean there is definitely a part of me that's curious about what that would feel like – to play those songs with those guys, to defy time and step back into former versions of ourselves.

"But I'm afraid of realizing that I haven't changed. That I haven't evolved; that I haven't faced anything or overcome anything. I mean – I've pretty much built my entire adult life on maintaining a vantage point that would spare me from having to look at those memories. Am I strong enough to face them now?"

She glanced up sideways at the silent, hovering mass of greens and browns.

"And then there's the whole issue of Michael Collins," she added. "Father Michael Collins."

She waited quietly, sitting cross-legged in the shade like Buddha. Ten minutes passed. No answer. Just as she was thinking about standing to leave, a new, warm wind blew through, and a green leaf fell slowly, tracing an erratic path through the air. It landed on her shoulder.

She decided to stay a little longer.

Edith lay awake taking an emotional inventory. So far, so good, she thought. She didn't detect an increase in anxiety, and her mood had, surprisingly, leveled a bit since she dumped the pills.

"See," she thought. "I really am better."

"It's my niece. I'm telling you. She is the queen of viral marketing. When this is all over, we so need to take her out to lunch."

Mandy had gone on a mission to Pittsburgh to turn the old Ghost Tree footage from analog to digital and to grab some more gear from a tech store there. Susan and Kenton were in Susan's room at the Cloverleaf, and Susan was giving her assessment of their uncanny marketing success thus far. The initial Ghost Tree video they'd posted had become the most watched clip on YouTube.

"That's amazing," Kenton said, still staring at the computer screen's 2,300,723 views. "What does that mean? Who are all those people and why do they even care about Ghost Tree?"

"Who the hell knows? I just know it means something's happening."

Susan was suddenly acutely aware of the attraction she felt for Kenton. It had been easily hidden before, with Mandy around more often than not and the three of them so busy they could barely catch a breath. But now, in this brief respite, alone in a motel room, she felt it as if it were a third person, sitting in the room with them.

"Let's play a game," she said, taking Kenton by the hand and leading him from the desk to the edge of the bed. "Okay?"

"Sure."

He sounded nervous. She loved that. She loved his wrinkled Green Day shirt and his thick, messy, brown hair.

"Okay. The game is called 'Tell Me When I'm Going to Fuck Up Either Our Project or Our Friendship.' The rules are simple. I move my hand to various places on your person, and you tell me the moment I'm about to fuck anything up."

"What are you…"

She covered his mouth and stopped him from completing his question.

"Does my hand on your mouth fuck up our friendship?" she asked, her breath suddenly competing with her voice to find space through her lips.

"No."

She moved her hand slowly and rested it, palm-down, on his chest. She felt his heart pounding. She loved his pounding heart, his piercing eyes, his racing brain. "You really don't know how irresistible you are, do you?' she thought, her nipples hardening as heat and light met to form wonderful humidity in her panties. The forecast definitely called for rain. She moved her hand down and rested it on his abdomen.

"Fucking up yet?"

"No."

Pinching the front of his T-shirt, she lifted him, as if by magic, to a stand. She remained seated – her head level with his waist. She rested four fingers on his belt buckle and looked up at him, the question implied in her smile.

"No," he whispered hoarsely.

Moments later Kenton stood naked from the waist down. He was beautiful. Susan could not remember being so completely drawn to a man. She wanted to eat him up, which was exactly what she planned to do.

"Am I fucking anything up?" she asked, her hand a fist now, moving with slow, firm deliberation as her lips moved closer.

"No," he croaked, then moaned as she tasted him for the first time.

5

Kenton: Do you remember the song *Mystic Light?*

Nathan: I do. I played it the other night. I wasn't getting the chords quite right; I was in a weird tuning. Still felt good.

Mandy: *(off camera)* I friggin' love that song. Your voice sounds friggin' awesome on it.

Nathan: Thanks. I always liked that one, too.

Kenton: How did you write that one?

Nathan: We all wrote it. The music we made in the barn kind of called the words out of me. We all wrote everything. Together.

Kenton: Have you been in any bands since then, Nathan?

Nathan: Yeah. A couple. I was in a disco band in Germany, believe it or not. And a country band in Texas. Old school country. Nothing ever felt like Ghost Tree, though.

Susan: How did Ghost Tree feel?

Nathan: Ghost Tree felt like being a kid in the middle of a field with a summer storm coming.

Kenton: So where have you been all these years?

Nathan: Germany. Texas. All over the place. I've been the classic drifter. Drifting here and drifting there. *(He pauses. Looks away.)* It's really not that interesting.

Kenton: Did you keep writing music?
Nathan: A little.

Susan: Did you keep in touch with any of your old band mates?
Nathan: No. I didn't. I saw Mike and Jane this past week. Hadn't seen either of them since I left town.

Kenton: Did you talk about the band?
Nathan: A little. We talked more about Chet.

Kenton: What do you remember about Chet?
Nathan: Just that he was the life of the party ... and never seemed to run out of ideas. He was a man with a plan.

Susan: Do you remember why Ghost Tree broke up, Nathan?
Nathan: (Pauses) Actually, we didn't, come to think of it. Jane left to go to Pittsburgh for school. And my dad was on me to join the army – which I did ... briefly.

Susan: Okay, Nathan. Here's the million-dollar question. Would you be willing to play a show with Ghost Tree?
Nathan: Yeah. I would.

"That guy is so friggin' hot."

Mandy spooned Campbell's soup into her mouth as she spoke. Kenton and Susan sat side by side on the bed's bottom edge. They were all in Mandy's room, a.k.a., the editing suite. A three-page deal memo from CBS lay behind them.

It was Sunday afternoon. Over the past two days the team had conducted dozens more interviews and spent long hours paring them down to what was most compelling in their collective opinion. They were working around the clock to complete a rough version of episode one, which they'd promised to get to Milo Lewis first thing the following morning.

Since Thursday's breakthrough with Susan, Kenton had barely slept. Between the work and the sex, there was just no time for it. And yet, he couldn't remember feeling quite so chipper.

"I'm thinking we get some of Nathan's interview in early," Mandy said. "He's the one that makes me want to keep watching."

"Are you thinking with your big head or your little head?" Susan asked.

"What? The guy is friggin' hot."

"I know he's hot," Susan said. "And I agree. He's got charisma to burn. We should definitely get him in early and often. I also love the stuff of his house. That's a cool-ass house."

Kenton found that he could focus on the interviews and the congealing footage for only so long before all thoughts were bumped by visions of Susan. *Susan in Ecstasy. Susan in Repose. Susan in Delight.* It was as if his brain were in constant preparation for a Susan Clawson exhibit. He focused now on *Susan Naked That Morning in the Shower,* and shifted a little on the bed. Susan smiled knowingly at him and reached back to grab the deal memo. She set it across his lap. She was easily the most amazing person he had ever met.

"Hey, Mandy," Susan said. "Kenton and I need to go over this contract before tomorrow. We're going to head over to my room."

"No worries. I'll just keep cutting up the stuff we all like so far. Should have something for you guys to look at in an hour or so."

An hour with Susan Clawson was an eternity. And yet, Kenton knew, it would pass in an instant. He was grateful that Susan stood first and then maintained a steady blockade of Mandy's view of him as he, the human tripod, stood and walked as best he could to the door.

Theresa Collins had prepared a roast. Mike, his older brother, Tim, and Tim's wife, Claudia, sat around the kitchen table, the head of which bore some type of child seat contraption for Mike's eighteen-month old nephew, Thaddeus, Mrs. Collins' lone grandchild.

"That's a good boy," she cooed to the smiling baby as he plucked dry Cheerios from his tray and placed them carefully in his mouth.

"He's not a dog, Mom," Tim said.

"Yeah, Mom, he's not a dog."

"I know he's not a dog," she defended before shifting back into pet-owner voice. "He's my good little boy."

Mike started laughing.

"So what's all this talk about your old band?" Claudia asked.

"Did you ever see us, Claud?" Mike asked. Claudia, too, was a life-long Pembrook resident. She and Tim had been high school sweethearts. Both had attended Slippery Rock University fifteen miles south, then married soon after graduation

"Of course," she said. "I think everyone in the whole town was at that Strawberry Days. You guys were awesome."

"Why thank you," Mike said in his very best Elvis. "Thank you very much."

"Funny how your imitations don't get any better over time," Tim observed. Mike sensed that his older brother was thinking about finger flicking Mike's left ear and shifted away ever so slightly.

"Are you guys going to play again?" Claudia asked. "I heard there's going to be a reunion concert in the field beside the Ghost Tree."

"News to me," Mike said. "All I know is that we're meeting out at Berg's tomorrow night to see what happens."

"Like with instruments and everything?" Tim said.

"Afraid so."

"Boy, could that Nathan ever sing," Mrs. Collins said.

The room fell silent as all eyes turned to her, surprised by the forceful opinion she'd offered.

"Since when are you an expert on Nathan's voice?" Tim asked.

"What? Can't a woman have an opinion? He could sing. That's all. Mike was always playing tapes in the house. I just paid attention, I suppose."

"I agree, mom," Claudia said. "Nathan could sing. And he wasn't hard to look at either."

Tim playfully punched his wife's upper arm, and the baby started crying in his mother's defense.

"It's okay," Tim said. "Mommy's not the floozy she makes herself out to be, son."

Mike laughed, ever grateful for the refuge of his family. Thankfully, the passing of his father seven years before had only strengthened the Collins' unity. He'd witnessed many cases in which just the opposite occurred.

"Want me to give you Nathan's number, mom?" Mike asked.

"Michael Collins. I expect better from a priest." She scooped mashed potatoes onto her plate, fighting a smile with each thick scoop. "By the way, they stopped to see me the other day."

"Who did?" Mike asked.

"Kenton and his friends. Isn't that tall girl pretty?"

"They stopped to see you?"

"Yes, me," she said. "Is that so hard to believe?"

"You're going to be a staaaar," Tim exclaimed. "My mom the movie staaaar."

"That Kenton is one thorough investigator," Mike said. "What kind of stuff did they ask?"

"Just what you'd expect, I suppose." She set down her fork and pushed her hair, more gray than black now, behind her left ear as she remembered the encounter. "The woman – was her name Susan? – asked about Jane a lot."

Mike took a break from eating and looked directly at his mom. He knew that just behind her June Cleaver demeanor there lurked a shrewd judge of character.

"What kind of stuff about Jane?"

"Oh, I don't know. She asked if you two were sweethearts."

"Jane and Mikey sitting in a tree," Tim sang. Years of training enabled Mike to ignore the tone-deaf chiding.

"What did you say?" Mike asked.

"I told them the truth, Michael. What do you think I said? I said you had been best friends since high school and never anything more than that." Mike went to ask more follow-up questions but was silenced by his mother's raised right index finger. "You'll just have to watch the movie," she added. "Mrs. Collins will be taking no further questions at the present time."

After Tim, Thad and Claudia left, Mike's melancholy returned.

"What's on your mind, honey?" Mrs. Collins asked, her motherly intuition in high gear as they washed the dishes.

"I'm having a little bit of a faith crisis, mom," he said, making it sound casual, a minor ailment along the lines of, say, a pesky cold.

"Isn't that pretty normal?" she asked. "I mean, don't you think every priest has moments of doubt? And don't you think that people in every line of work sometimes doubt their choice, or feel a little lost?" She set down her dishrag and looked directly at her son. "Can I tell you something I've never told anyone?"

"You didn't kill anyone or anything, did you?"

"No, silly. But I almost felt like I had."

Mike stopped his cleaning duty, too, to give his mother his full attention.

"When your father and I had been married for about twelve years, I woke up one morning and felt like I didn't even know him. Nothing had changed. We were just a husband and wife waking to face another day in the world, but…"

"What?"

"He was an absolute stranger, right then. It terrified me. I faked my way through, but privately I went into a pretty dark place there. Doubting. Questioning. Desperate for solid ground. Sound familiar?"

Mike nodded.

"Thank God, I was patient with myself and with the man I loved. And within a month or so it all receded, and I came to value our marriage, and all of you, even more." She placed a hand on Mike's forearm. "So doubting can be good, honey. Productive, even. Just be patient with yourself."

"How'd you get to be so wise?"

"I got old."

Driving home later, he remembered the way she had smiled and how her eyes had held the pain she saw in his. Was such acute empathy typical of all mothers, he wondered? How devastated would she be if he failed to stay the course, and chose to leave the priesthood? How crushed would she be to know that his moment of doubt was as much about Jane Taylor as it was about theology?

As the fall of evening's darkness became more than just a pale idea, Nathan Booth paused his pacing to light some candles. Ghost Tree songs played through the ancient boom box. He'd been listening all day. With the candles now ablaze, he clicked off the music and sat at the table. He grabbed his guitar, and the music poured out of him.

Susan: Thanks for letting us invade your house like this, Mrs. Collins.

Theresa Collins: Don't even think of it. I don't get too many surprises, and this is a nice one. It's always nice to see you, Kenton.

Kenton: It's good to see you too, Mrs. Collins. Have you heard about what we're doing?

Theresa: Of course. Everyone in town has heard. You're doing a movie about Michael's old band.

Susan: We're trying to get them to play together again. Do you think that would be a good idea?

Theresa: I have mixed feelings about it.

Susan: Care to elaborate?

Theresa: Well, on one hand, I firmly believe that you can't go back in time. As you get older, like me, you wish more and more that you could sometimes. But you can't. So when I see people trying to, I have some misgivings.

Susan: But?

Theresa: But on the other hand, I don't think I ever saw my son as happy as he was when he was making music with that band. We only saw their very last performance ...

Mandy: Strawberry Days.

Theresa: Yes, Strawberry Days. But it was like I was watching some-one else's eighteen-year old. He was transformed. Michael was always a bit of an introvert. Friendly enough, but self-conscious and just a little reserved. But that day it was like he was a carefree little boy again. *(Pauses. Sips her tea.)* I actually remember thinking that I hoped he would pursue it instead of attending college. *(She laughs.)* Can you be-lieve that? A mother hoping her son doesn't go to college.

Susan: Makes you a good mom, in my book.

Theresa: Why thank you. Turned out to be a moot point. They nev-er played again after that.

Susan: Were Mike and Jane ever an item?

Theresa: *(Looks surprised)* No. They weren't. They were insepara-ble, pretty much, but never a couple. They were something better – best friends.

Susan: Did you ever wish they were an item?

Theresa: No. I didn't. I didn't think of it. I was always glad he had such a great friend.

Kenton: Do you remember if Mike told you why the band stopped playing?

Theresa: I only remember being dissatisfied with whatever reason he gave. If you could have seen them that day ... their last per-formance ... and seen the way people reacted to what they were doing ... you would have thought they'd go on play-ing forever. So it was very strange when they just stopped.

Susan: Jane and Nathan weren't a couple, were they?

Theresa: I don't think so. Though, they could have been, and I might not have known about it. I probably wouldn't have, as a matter of fact. Mothers never do.

Susan: Why do you think they pulled the plug?

Theresa: Michael said something about Jane's parents insisting she go to college as planned. Of course, all the kids had plans right then. So it wasn't the best timing in the world. It could have been that simple.

Susan: But?

Theresa: Jane was such a strong-minded young woman. And though I knew her parents had strong opinions about things, I just had the sense that she would make her own choice regarding the band.

Susan: So you thought there was more to it.

Theresa: Yes. I did. But I didn't pry.

"I really like that woman," Susan said. Mandy's room had the messy, manic feel of a college kid's dorm room at finals time. Susan loved the non-stop, manic energy that accompanied a project like this – a project fueled by collaboration, and synchronicity, and fate, and now, head-over-heels love.

"Me, too," Mandy replied. "Cool lady."

"What are you thinking about all that?" Kenton asked. "Why were you asking all those questions about Jane."

"My spider sense is telling me there's something big we don't know – a love triangle or something like that? Maybe Jane fell in love with someone, and someone else was wishing it was him. Or maybe Jane loved someone who didn't love her back. You know what they say? Never put a chick in the band. Recipe for disaster."

Kenton nodded. Damn, was he ever adorable. Her mind flashed on their most recent escapade. The frantic desperation was fading a little as their bodies fatigued, and their awareness became just slightly less brand new. He was more tender with her than she'd been expecting. It was disarming, really, and a total turn-on. Nobody had ever looked in her eyes the way he had … with such unabashed need. The man was not afraid of being vulnerable, and it made Susan vulnerable. Who knew vulnerability could feel so good?

"Whatever you say, boss," he said with a weary smile.

She went over to the sink where he stood and took his hand in hers. She lifted it to her lips and kissed the soft skin. "Kenton and I are an item," she announced to Mandy.

Mandy studied them. Her nose and mouth scrunched into a curious smile. "Really? Didn't see that one coming."

"Just wanted to get that out into the open. We take a solemn oath not to let our personal shenanigans interfere with this historic project, though. Isn't that right, Kenton?"

"That's right. We won't let you down, Mandy."

"Guys, I'm just grateful to be here. Do you know how totally fun this all is? You letting me down is not exactly high on my list of worries."

Susan was filled with a sense of total love – for Kenton, for Mandy, for Pembrook, for America, for the world, for the universe. She also realized that she could really stand to get some sleep.

What a strange time, Jane thought as she pulled away from the coffee shop Sunday night. Nothing could have prepared her for the events of the past couple of weeks. She turned right onto Broad Street and drove the half mile to Saint Luke's.

"Hey," she said as Mike let her in through the rectory's back kitchen door.

"Hey yourself."

"Ready to rehearse for rehearsal?"

"Ready as I'll ever be."

She lugged her gear into the rectory's cozy living room. Mike's bass leaned against the sofa.

"I'm surprised you still have that."

She pointed to the tall Ampeg amplifier that stood in the corner.

"It was in my mom's basement. Still sounds awesome, by the way."

"I always loved that thing. I have no idea if my stuff will even work. I haven't played through it in forever."

After powering up, plugging in, and tuning their instruments the two friends sat on opposite ends of the couch, their respective amplifiers at their sides. The small lamp on the table at Jane's end cast the room's only light. Mike pressed play and *Mystic Light* from twenty years ago surrounded them.

Jane's brain struggled to remind her fingers where they were supposed to be on the fret board. Slowly the patterns returned and her present-day self started echoing the rhythm parts her eighteen-year-old self had played. It felt oddly second-nature, as if she'd played the song two months not two decades ago.

As she eased deeper into the music and began to trust in her knowledge of it, she closed her eyes and let the images play. She saw them all in the barn as the summer nights fell, and the sound of their songs became all that there was. She saw Kenny smiling with his eyes closed, his arms and legs flailing. She saw Jonathon looking so serious as he concentrated on staying with the others no matter what occurred. She saw Nathan, trancelike and lost behind his guitar and his microphone. She saw Mike standing beside Kenny, the bass line seeming to fall straight out of the kick drum.

It all came back to her with this music she had held so dearly, this music that simply couldn't be a bad thing, even if it was twenty years too late. With her eyes still closed, she saw a dozen other roads rolling out from that point and wondered why she chose the loneliest one. The weight of that loneliness fell on her now, her spirit exhausted from all the years of feigned sturdiness. As the song ended, a tear fell across her red guitar, and she realized it had come from her.

"Are you okay, Jane?"

For once she didn't force her way back up to solid ground. She let herself crumble. A drop became a river, and before she knew what was happening Mike's arms were around her, and she was safe against his chest. She clasped a hand onto a wrist behind his back and pulled him close as she finally allowed herself to cry.

Susan: How was it having a girl in the band?

Kenny: Jane? It was cool.

Susan: No one had a crush on her or anything?

Kenny: I didn't say that. I actually think Chet had a pretty big crush on her … and maybe Mike. Hell, Nathan did too for all I know. She's a cool, pretty girl.

Susan: What about you? Did you have a crush on Jane?

Kenny: No. I'm lucky that way. I hardly ever want things I know I can't have.

Kenton: Have you played drums all your life?

Kenny: Pretty much. My dad was a drummer.

Kenton: I didn't know that.

Kenny: Yeah. A good one, too. And he really encouraged me to get into it. And once I did he was always willing to help me lug my gear all around.

Susan: Nice.

Kenny: He was Ghost Tree's roadie. Chet helped. But my dad made sure we all got to the gigs and told all the other parents he'd look out for us, which he did. *(Long pause.)* He died last year. Did you know he died, Kenton?

Kenton: I heard that, man. I'm really sorry.

Kenny: Cancer. Wish he could have lived to see all this stuff happening.

Susan: You mean the Ghost Tree stuff?

Kenny: Yeah. He loved us. And my dad was pretty much exclusively into jazz. So for him to like what we did was saying something.

Susan: Why do you think he liked it so much?

Kenny: I think just because it was original. He said he hadn't heard anything like it. I think he was expecting us to play Allman

Brothers covers like every other band that ever existed around here.

Kenton: Would you say there was a jazz influence with Ghost Tree? You wouldn't call yourself a jazz drummer would you?

Kenny: No way. I'm not good enough. But I think the band had a jazz spirit. We were all about the moment and wrote as we played. I've never worked with people like that again.

"Can you go straight from that into *Blast Away?*" Kenton asked. He was referring to one of the more improvisational Ghost Tree songs. "We have some great footage of them working on that one, don't we?"

Mandy's fingers sped across the keypad as she scanned the rehearsal footage to find the song. The three agreed in silent unison that the drummer's words would fit nicely behind it.

"I just got chills for about the thousandth time," Susan said. "Nice work, Mandy."

"Yeah," Kenton agreed. "Nice work. So where does that leave us?"

"I should have a rough version of forty-two minutes by about midnight."

"And we're all agreed that we'll hold off on asking for another crew from CBS?" Susan clarified. "At least for the time being?"

"Agreed," confirmed Mandy. "My friend Trey is coming up from Pittsburgh and bringing a couple of assistants tomorrow to help us get some more angles on the rehearsal. That should cover us for now."

Susan told Mandy that was perfect and that she and Kenton were going to try and sleep a little, but would be back at midnight. Then the couple went outside. The office light was on. Susan knew that Lou would be in there watching his programs. It seemed every time she passed there was a version of *Law and Order* on the tube. The man liked his crime drama.

"How you feeling?" she asked.

"I'm feeling as good as I've ever felt in my whole life," Kenton said.

"Ghost Tree good, or us good?"

"Both."

She was a good three inches taller than he was, which she was surprised didn't bother her. If they'd been the same height, his intensity might have scared her off. At least looking down at him gave her some sense of control, albeit, a false one.

"Me, too," she said.

"We should try to sleep a little," he suggested.

"I know. It's starting to hit me. Together or alone?"

"Together," he said.

"Your place or mine?"

"Yours."

"I like a man who can make a decision."

As they walked she continued thinking about Jane, Mike, and Nathan. They entered her room and she said, "I know there's something more there, Kenton ... with Jane, I mean. I should try to talk to her off camera sometime ... woman to woman. Maybe tomorrow night I can take her aside or figure out some way to make that happen."

"That sounds good ... and I'm sure you're right. Maybe we should contact her folks, too. I think they're living in Florida. I'll try and do that first thing in the morning."

"Perfect," she said. "Now shut up and kiss me, then let's pass out."

"It's a good kind of tired," Mandy muttered. She sat alone in her room, staring at the computer screen for the eighth hour in a row. She meant it. It was the kind of tired that came from doing something you loved. And she loved this project. She loved Kenton and Susan. She loved the freedom they were giving her to get things how she wanted them in terms of the "look" of it all. She loved the thought of the big paycheck Kenton had mentioned she'd be receiving when they were through. And she genuinely loved the band (especially that singer – God Almighty, was he hot.) She had stumbled into the dream gig for which she had been waiting all her life. And she was enjoying every minute of it.

She went back to an interview she'd edited earlier in the evening – the one they'd done the previous afternoon with Jane Taylor. She didn't know why, but she felt drawn to the woman. Maybe it was her classic American-girl good looks ... dimpled cheeks and curly brown hair. Or maybe it was the sadness Mandy recognized in the café manager's eyes. She wasn't sure what it was, exactly, which was why she cued it up again just after Kenton and Susan left the room…

Susan: Do you still have that cool red guitar?

Jane: Sure do. Haven't played it in a long, long time, but every now and then I open the case to make sure it's still there.

Susan: That doesn't look like the kind of guitar an eighteen year old should be playing. Where did you get it?

Jane: My dad's brother – Uncle Charlie. He was the black sheep of the family. They were all straight-laced conservative Christian types and, by their standards, Uncle Charlie was a true subversive – all about old Blues and Rock-and-Roll. He chose me to pass the torch to. He was always taking me for rides with him, and playing me devil's music like Robert Ronson and Muddy Waters, and old Rolling Stones, and Van Morrison. And he'd tell me all his stories about playing on the road ... which was what he did before he gave up and became an insurance agent in Sharon. I think he was hoping he could live through me since he wasn't doing it any more.

Susan: Is he still around?

Jane: Actually, he is. My mom and dad moved to Florida after my dad retired, and most of the rest of the family followed. But Uncle Charlie still lives in Sharon.

Susan: Was he a Ghost Tree fan?

Jane: Absolutely.

Susan: Nice.

Kenton: I remember your Uncle Charlie. What kind of car did he drive?

Jane: He somehow came into possession of a bright red 1956 Austin Healy. Don't know what it was with him and the color red. That and the Rickenbacker were his prized possessions. Sometimes wish he'd given me the car and not the guitar. It was a seriously cool car.

Susan: Were you warned about this interview? Were you dreading it?

Jane: Mike mentioned that I might be hearing from you. I wouldn't say I was dreading it. Though who really wants to see themselves on camera?

Susan: You mean other than pretty much everybody?

Jane: Yeah. Other than them.

Kenton: Do you remember how Ghost Tree formed. Who put it all together?

Jane: Chet did. He was the kind of guy who knew everybody – even Nathan … which was no easy thing. Nathan was not exactly accessible.

Susan: Can you tell us what you mean by that … about Nathan?

Jane: He just kind of marched to his own drum, you know. I actually think Chet just happened to hear Nathan singing somehow … when Nathan thought he was alone. Chet had this instant vision of a band and kind of ran with it.

Susan: So Chet heard Nathan singing to himself then ran to you and Mike?

Jane: Pretty much. And he sold Mike and me on the idea … Chet was a persuasive guy. Then Mike and I went back and talked to Nathan about forming a band and, surprisingly, he was into the idea. Jonathon and Kenny were pretty much the only other players we knew in the school – so they were no-brainers. What we didn't know was how eerily compatible we'd all be in terms of our tastes, and our style, and all that. We all loved the same bands. The Replacements, the Waterboys, the Silos.

Susan: And you felt right away like you guys had the same kind of special sauce as those bands did?

Jane: Most definitely. We were awesome. By the way, Kenton, we all totally knew you were spying on rehearsals. I think we kinda liked having an audience.

Susan: So why didn't you stick with it, Jane? What happened at the end of that summer ... after Strawberry Days, I mean?

Jane: Well as I'm sure you heard from the others, I kind of pulled the plug on things. My dad had already put money down for Pitt, and he wasn't exactly the kind of guy to be swayed by rock-and-roll dreams. I guess you could say he put his foot down.

Kenton: How did you let the other guys know?

Jane: I've always regretted the way it happened. I was just so upset about the whole turn of events that I couldn't deal. I told Mike and asked him to let the others know. And that was the end of it.

Susan: Then you went to Pitt.

Jane: Briefly. I dropped out after the first year. I actually thought Ghost Tree might be able to pick up where we left off, but Nathan was long gone by then and everybody else had settled onto a different path. It was kind of ironic. I was the one who pulled the plug, and I wound up being the one wanting most to try again ... only it was too late. Nathan only came back in the past year. And, to be honest, I hadn't even thought about the band in a long, long time.

Susan: Well, I think you know the question that's coming.

Jane: Hit me with it.

Susan: Would you be willing to do one more show with your old
            band, Ghost Tree.

Jane: I'm amazed to report that I would be willing to do that, in
            memory of Chet Howard. *(Straight to the camera.)* Chet, if
            you're watching this, forgive us if we suck.

Kenny Maxim stood in the kitchen of his small one-story house.
Sweat dripped from his face and arms as he reached into the refrigerator and grabbed the carton of orange juice, from which he took
several long gulps.

He looked out the window. It was another beautiful May night in
Pembrook – a rare night off for him. Between the five local bands
he drummed with, he was always playing somewhere. He'd happily
dropped everything for the Ghost Tree reunion, though. Those
other bands could fire him for all he cared. He'd needed a break or
a change or something, anyway. He couldn't believe he'd be getting
another chance to play those songs. Life amazed him sometimes.

He went back into the living room where he had his practice kit
set up. He sat down behind it and put his headphones on. *She Took
the Key* piped through his eardrums, straight into his brain, and
he reacted first with his feet, keeping time and pressing hard and
steady on the kick drum pedal, then next with his arms as they or-
chestrated their wild assault on his battery of drums and cymbals.
He smiled like a child as he played the old songs. It was exactly like
riding a bike, he thought, only downhill and two hundred miles
per hour.

The Krings had left their giant Plymouth Roadmaster in the garage and urged the girls to feel free to use it. Molly generally stuck
with the "shoe-leather express," uncomfortable with the vehicle's
unwieldy length and girth, but Edith had taken to driving through

Pembrook most evenings, sometimes until very late at night … just thinking.

Sunday, she had been parked a block away from the coffee shop at closing time and squinted to see Jane emerge eventually, lock the front door, and walk to her car. At a distance, Edith followed her down Main Street and onto Broad and watched as her beautiful employer pulled into Saint Luke's. Edith waited on the street for a few minutes, then entered the lot and parked in the very last row to keep watch.

She didn't drink coffee, had never been allowed to because of the medication, but had become addicted of late to Mountain Dew, a half-empty twelve-pack of which sat in the car's spacious back seat area. She complemented the steady stream of the sweet caffeinated beverage with a diet of Mike and Ikes and Hot Tomales. The caffeine and sugar combination kept her awake and alert.

Hours passed. Edith sipped her soda and chewed her candy as she watched the building's entrance. Jane never came out.

Each night, Jonathon and Carol Hilliard knelt and prayed, side by side. It had gotten to where they couldn't sleep without this phase of their ritual. Sunday night was no different. Their elbows touched on the bed as each silently reflected on the day's events.

"Can I say something?" Jonathon asked, still on his knees.

"You may," she said softly as her prayer time ended.

"I need to forgive Jane. I think I've been angry with her all these years. And if I'm honest with myself, I actually make a point of avoiding her whenever possible. I think I really felt like she robbed us all of a dream back then."

Carol nodded.

"And now that the dream is kind of reappearing, I'm realizing that this resentment is tainting everything."

"Just talk to her, Jon. One honest conversation and that can all disappear. It will all disappear."

"I know you're right," he said. "I just needed to say it out loud to get the ball rolling, I think."

"Now can I tell you something?"

"Of course."

"I'm a little scared about all this Ghost Tree stuff. I know we don't really know what it is yet, but I'm afraid it's going to take you away from us. I'm not really sure I want you becoming a rock star at the age of thirty-eight, with three kids counting on you being here for them."

Jonathon smiled as they stood, and then sat on the edge of the bed. "Listen, Carol," he said, "if, by some miracle, I do get to play rock star for a minute, I'll make sure my family shares the ride." With the index finger of his right hand he lifted her chin, forcing more direct eye contact. "Scout's honor."

He pulled her close for a goodnight kiss.

Kenton:	Thanks for talking with us again, Fay.
Fay:	No problem, sweetie. What else does an old bird like me have to do?
Susan:	Don't sell yourself short, Fay. You seem to be the hardest working woman in Pembrook.
Fay:	I'd hardly call it work. I basically get paid to talk. Don't tell anyone.
Susan:	Speaking of talking, do you talk much with Jane Taylor?
Fay:	Every chance I get. I love that girl.
Susan:	Can you tell me more about her?
Fay:	What do you want to know?
Susan:	What was she like back then? Has she changed much since high school?
Fay:	Haven't we all? I weighed 125 pounds and had real red hair in high school. *(Pause.)* She and Mike would stop in the Donut Shack after their band practices that summer. I felt like I was sitting inside a constellation or something,

they were so lit up with everything. It was something to see, let me tell you.

Kenton: Did Jane seem different after she came back from Pittsburgh?

Fay: Yeah, I guess she did ... at least for a while. I remember hearing she was home, but hadn't seen her myself, so I was a little worried about her. We had bonded pretty good in those late night talks. She held a special place for me. When she finally stopped by, I think I did notice a little of the light gone from her eyes. I just thought the big city beat her up a little. But before long, she was her old self again.

Susan: I'm surprised she's not married. She's beautiful, smart, funny. Has she ever had a steady boyfriend or a fiancé or anything like that?

Fay: I think Jane shares my sense that men are fun to have around but not to tie you down. It took me three husbands to reach that conclusion – so more power to Jane for sparing herself the suffering. She and Father Mike sometimes talk like they're a married couple, but that's just because they've been friends so long.

Susan had dozed for a few minutes, but couldn't seem to give herself over to dreamland. Ghost Tree songs and interview clips cycled through her brain. Kenton slept peacefully at her side. He even snored cute.

Something was bothering her.

It was Jane Taylor. Jane just didn't add up for Susan. She was clearly a bright, funny, and very attractive woman, but she'd never had a serious boyfriend. She'd loved the band as much as the rest of them did, and yet had let it go without even a final meeting. Susan just knew there was something more there ... something hidden, or buried.

In the same way that Susan knew she would one day make babies with the sweet, sexy, clueless man sleeping at her side, so, too, did she know that the mystery of Ghost Tree was the mystery of Jane. Solve one and you've solved them both.

6

The sound of the fax machine awakened Milo Lewis just before dawn Monday morning. After working through the weekend, he had slept on his plush, black, office couch. Office sleep-overs always seemed to bring good luck. This one was no exception. He jumped up and ran out to find the final page of the signed Ghost Tree deal memo churning its way from Pembrook to New York City. At the top, Susan Clawson had printed, "Don't make us regret this, Milo!" Milo smiled.

Back in his office, he awakened his sleeping desktop screen. As expected, there was an email from Susan in his inbox, directing Milo to Mandy Lewis' personal file server. After several mouse clicks, he was downloading a rough cut of episode one. As the massive file came through, he rushed into his private bathroom, stripped and showered, then threw on fresh jeans and a clean white T- shirt. Looking in the mirror he decided that his gray hair and casual attire gave him the look of an aging British rocker – one, perhaps, who'd recently been knighted. The thought brought a small smile.

He hurried back out to his computer. The download was complete. Doing his best to clear his mind of expectation, Milo pressed the space bar and began to watch. Forty-two minutes later, his face hurt from smiling. There was literally nothing he didn't like about what he had just seen. The look was natural, and felt real in a way he hadn't seen on prime-time television. The town and its people were humble and honest and funny … and he wanted more. Susan and Kenton were an oddly appealing pair of hosts; his quirkiness and her beauty somehow complementing each other. And the music, well, the music was the real kicker – it was simply stunning. He felt like he'd been watching a documentary about the birth of some legendary band. Sure, the whole thing needed some sprucing up before its final, national presentation. In general, though, it was perfect.

Whatever Susan and her team were doing, he was going to be damn sure not to screw it up. Sometimes being a good leader meant knowing when not to lead. This was clearly one of those times. He decided on impulse to go tell them in person how thrilled he was with the way things were shaping up. He would call his travel agent and book a flight – right after he woke up his friend, Stan Markham, one of the movers-and-shakers at Columbia Records.

The Taylors were a dead end. Kenton had found their Florida phone number and had already given them a call. Though Jane's mother did, in fact, remember the band, the memories didn't seem to be fond ones. Regarding Jane's band-breaking trip to Pittsburgh, she confirmed that her daughter had just been following through with the plans that were already in place, and that Mrs. Taylor and her husband didn't deem a rock band worthy of altering the girl's life course.

"She definitely didn't want to talk about it," Kenton said over a table filled with syrup-soaked chocolate-chip pancakes, peppered, scrambled eggs and pots of strong black coffee. The Pembrook Diner was jumping.

Mandy had a camera set up near their table and was capturing the strategy session, as she did pretty much all of the trios conversations. Kenton and Susan barely even noticed any more, which was why they were turning out to be such natural 'hosts.' The three conspirators had viewed the rough cut of episode one the night before.

Susan was surprised by how good it felt to see a close-to-finished version of their work.

"Have I mentioned how perfect the rough cut looked?" she asked, her mouth filled with egg.

"I believe you did say something to that effect."

"Really, Mandy. You are killing this thing."

Kenton nodded yes to Fay's extra napkin offer. Susan watched as he wiped egg from his chin. Sunlight bathed the scene and seemed to fuel the warmth that swelled in her chest. Susan was grateful to have made it to a place in her life where she didn't fight happiness.

"If Milo can't see how awesome it is, he doesn't deserve us anyway."

"Who's Milo?" This question came from Fay, whom Susan now viewed as a trusted friend.

"He's head of programming at CBS," she answered.

"So our little town is really going to be on national television?"

Susan knew that whatever Fay discerned in that moment would be relayed ad infinitum, and didn't mind in the least. She thought the natives' reactions were an important element of what they were doing. The more they could give people to react to, the better. "That's the plan, Fay. You okay with that?"

"Hell yes," the woman of undetermined hair color replied, then added, "We could use a little shaking up around here," before proceeding to the next table in her station.

"Have you heard back from him yet?" Mandy asked.

"No. I just sent the email and the fax a couple of hours ago. He's probably not in the office yet. You know those cushy executive types."

"Do I ever? I almost married one."

Susan found Mandy's carefully constructed life history, one that omitted her homosexuality, fascinating. Of course, Susan had been wrong before. She had half-thought Milo was gay, if memory served. He wasn't.

"And you'll try and talk with Jane tonight?" asked Kenton.

"Yeah, if it's possible. Is anybody else as excited about tonight as I am?"

"Yeah," Kenton admitted. "It will be a real blast from the past for me. I'm pretty stoked."

"Me, too," Mandy said. "It'll be fun to have some help, too. You guys are gonna like my friend from Pittsburgh."

"When will he be here?" Kenton asked.

"He's actually bringing a little crew with him. I'm supposed to meet them at Micky D's at three, then lead them out to Berg's. It'll take us a few hours to get all set up."

They talked and they ate for an hour longer. Though Susan didn't mention it, she wondered why Milo hadn't called. It wasn't like him to delay.

"What are you listening to, Sam?"

Jonathon Hilliard asked this question of his teenaged daughter as she joined him Monday morning at the kitchen counter. She couldn't hear him over the sound of her song, and didn't answer. Jonathon felt like it had been years since any of his kids heard him the first time he said something. He pushed Sam's upper arm, and she cast him an irritated glance as she pulled out the small white iPod headphones.

"What, dad?" she asked, already exasperated.

"What are you listening to?"

They reached simultaneously for a carton of Raisin Bran. Jonathon acquiesced and waited as she poured a helping into her cereal bowl.

"Plain White Ts," she said.

"Give me that." He grabbed the headphones and placed them in his ears. She pressed the play button and stood patiently as he sampled the song while pouring his own cereal portion.

"It's okay, I guess," he said, as he returned her listening apparatus. "Although, they're really just ripping off music from twenty-five years ago."

"Isn't everybody just ripping something off from another time?"

They sat across from one another at the brown, circular kitchen table, which had played host to thousands of such breakfast conversations. Debating was a favorite pastime for Jonathon and his eldest daughter. They debated everything from future colleges to Steelers' player personnel. It probably explained why they remained so close when it was more like pulling teeth getting his other kids to engage in intelligent conversation.

"That's a good point," Jonathon conceded. "But I think when you draw from the past you should make it your own in a way that's interesting, and kind of distinct to who you are. I'm not sure I hear that in the Stained White Tease."

"Plain White T-s," she corrected, with the combination of love and disdain that seemed always to define her end of their dialogues. "And if you don't know anything about where it comes from, and have nothing to compare it with, then who cares? I like it."

"Another valid point." Jonathon suppressed the urge to reach across and push the brown hair from his daughter's expressive brown eyes. He was amazed, sometimes, by how much like an infant she still felt to him. Where did all the time go? "So, do you have that band's CD?"

"No," Sam said. "I just downloaded that song 'cause I heard it on a TV show."

"And will you ever buy their record?"

"Probably not."

"When I was your age if someone turned me on to something and I loved it, I couldn't sleep until I had the record in my hands and was scouring the liner notes. You had to work for things, Sam. You couldn't just click a button then have it that instant so that you could forget about it ten minutes later. It involved effort, and choices, and commitment. So when you decided to get into something, you really got into it."

His voice had risen in the course of his speech. He saw an all-too familiar smile appear on his lone audience member's face, a smile containing one part love and three parts, dismissal.

"When's your big rehearsal?" Sam asked, conveniently ignoring his last volley.

"Tonight." He shrugged, her mysterious ways beyond his comprehension. "We're meeting out at Berg's at six o'clock."

"Are you nervous?"

"Yeah. To be honest, I'm really nervous. I could hardly sleep last night."

"Will you remember the songs? I really like that one on YouTube, by the way. I scored major points with all my friends. You guys were pretty good."

"I know we were. Maybe that's why I'm nervous. I'm afraid we won't be now, and it might kind of cancel the memory out and remind us of our age. I'm also a little nervous about remembering my parts and dusting off my chops and all that."

"Are you interested in getting some advice from a fifteen year old?"

"Always."

"Play from your heart and you can't go wrong. A wise man once told me that before a championship soccer match."

"You're pretty great. You know that, Sam?"

"You're pretty great yourself. Mind if I tag along to the rehearsal?"

"Not at all," Jonathon replied, amazed by his daughter's interest.

Ghost Tree chatter was steady and strong, each new Steerbuck's customer providing some fresh detail or perspective. Edith felt the electricity in the air. Something was happening.

"Did you hear that Kenton Hall is dating that pretty woman he's working with?" Donna Hillbeck asked. "Talk about a mismatch."

"Nathan Booth's been in prison for the past twenty years for shooting a man from Slippery Rock in a bar fight. My cousin Pepper saw the whole thing." That one came from Mrs. Greely, the town's lone librarian.

"They're playing a free concert in Mischeler's field," Julie Chetlin had announced.

"Really?" Edith asked as she made change for the thirty-something beautician.

"This coming Saturday. It's going to be on MTV."

"MTV?" Edith asked, a hint of skepticism in her voice. "I thought CBS was doing it."

"Nope. MTV. Tom at the gas station told me."

Another customer insisted that Jane had disappeared. Jane's absence that morning only strengthened the allegation. Edith had nipped that one in the bud, assuring the earnest customer that Jane had simply taken the day off. And who could blame her? Even the most levelheaded woman would have trouble dealing.

And yet, Edith, who was operating on roughly forty-five minutes of sleep, which came behind the wheel of the Kring's car in the Saint Luke's parking lot, felt strangely invigorated by it all. History was happening, history she was part of in some small way. The only question remaining was: where would it all end? Edith, for one, couldn't wait to find out.

She steadied her hands and focused on the matters at hand. Making drinks. Counting change. Being normal.

Jane was gone. She'd still been sleeping on the couch when Mike left for morning mass but was gone when he returned. In truth, he was glad. He wasn't sure he could face her with the memory of the previous night still fresh.

He'd held her as she cried and whispered quietly that she would be okay, that everything was all right. No words had accompanied her tears, so he was still in the dark about the exact nature of her burden, but he was grateful for the comfort she had allowed him to offer. He grimaced now, remembering the way his concern had shifted to something different – need … desire – as her sobs subsided and she fell to sleep in his arms. He had savored the feeling of stroking her hair before gently easing her down, looking too long, covering her in blankets. He'd left her to her dreams but returned later wanting to hold her again, to feel her again, to breathe in her scent again. He had sat on the chair and watched her sleep, then finally forced himself to go off and search for his own fitful dreams.

He stood now in the center of the living room, relief and disappointment jockeying for position within him. He picked up the phone and called his friend, Father William O'Shea.

"Bill," he began, his voice steadier than expected, "I have some kind of crazy news."

"What is it, lad?"

The booming question was filled with familiar friendliness, but Mike wasn't quite buying it. Mike sensed that the older priest knew what was coming.

"Remember how you're always talking about dark nights of the soul?"

"Of course, Michael. Everybody needs at least one."

"Well, I've had about fifty in a row. And I've decided I need to take a sabbatical. I might even be leaving the priesthood."

Mike's heart raced as the words poured out. He told his friend everything as, for the first time, his secret heart was given voice.

"I'm in love with her, Bill. I think I've been in love with her all my life. I think I might even have become a priest to help convince myself that I wasn't in love with her, but I'm just not able to ignore it any longer."

There was silence on the line. Finally the older priest spoke. "I have to tell you I'm very saddened to hear this, Mike. Do you understand the severity of what you're considering? How would you counsel a couple that came to you with similar struggles regarding their marriage?"

"I'd tell them that their vows were sacred and that they should proceed very cautiously."

"Exactly," Father Bill interrupted. "And you have to consider yourself a spouse here. You took vows ... you married your faith, essentially. And you can't let go of that commitment lightly."

"This isn't a casual decision," Mike said defensively. "And, truth be told, if I spent time with an unhappy couple and determined that real happiness wasn't a possibility in their situation, I'd accept divorce."

"Then you're not the priest I thought you were," Bill replied, as close to anger as Mike had ever heard him.

"I think that's my point."

Milo Lewis and Stan Markham sat side by side in the first class section of USAirways Flight 1325 from New York to Pittsburgh. Stanley had downloaded the file Milo had directed him to, and was grateful his friend had clued him in. Ghost Tree was, indeed, something special. And though normally the ages of the band members, somewhere north of thirty-five, would have precluded his interest, the ready-made promotional campaign made that something of a moot point. And, anyway, there really weren't any rules anymore – at least not rules that he could decipher.

"To Ghost Tree," Stan said, lifting the can of Diet Coke the flight attendant had just placed on his tray table.

"To Ghost Tree," Milo echoed, lifting his Diet Sprite and taking a sip.

"That You Tube thing was pretty amazing too, huh?" Stan recognized the sound of thrilled opportunism in his own voice. It had been a long time. And he couldn't deny that there had been something in the Ghost Tree music, something more than the typical *"This is okay, I can probably make money from this"* reaction. He saw himself in the clips of the band from way back when. It called to mind his teenaged years in upstate New York, discovering his older brother's Todd Rundgren and Ian Hunter records – discovering himself in the center of a million songs. It was hard to stay connected to that part of his soul, the part that had led him into this line of work – work which had become so much more about business than music.

"I know it," Milo agreed. "The whole thing is pretty amazing. I feel like we're on a mission to correct history or something. Like this band was destined for greatness but got derailed through some trick of fate, and we have to make it right."

"So tell me the whole story again."

Milo happily recounted, knowing that the story was everything. The 'story' could determine whether a project flew or crashed. He started with Susan Clawson ("the most beautiful woman I have ever had an actual conversation with") and went from there, concluding with the fax and the file he received that morning.

"How much do I love you for calling me, Milo? I owe you one, brother." He took off his wire-rimmed glasses and rubbed his eyes more out of habit than fatigue. He set the glasses down and scratched at the gristle of his goatee – another habit. "Do you think they'll have any idea how lucky they are?"

"Based on my conversations with Susan, not really."

"Bummer."

As Jane drove, she struggled to push away the sensory memory of Mike's T-shirt as it had felt against her cheek and the faint scent of Old Spice it held. After stopping for coffee at the one-pump Texaco that stood all alone on one of the more desolate stretches of Route 29, she turned right up Mountain Road. According to Mike, Nathan lived about seven miles up the hill.

She turned tentatively onto the nearly-hidden dirt road that led to his house and was relieved to find him sitting on the front steps of his porch, strumming a black acoustic guitar. She wasn't sure she'd have found the nerve to ring the doorbell, if it had come to that.

"Hey," he said, as she walked from her jeep to the foot of the wooden steps.

"Hey," she said. "Cool house." She looked up at the oddly angled wooden edifice – amazed at how like its owner it was … beautiful and enigmatic. "How is it you manage not to have to work for a living?"

He smiled as he lifted his right hand from the guitar's sound hole to his head and finger-combed his long, dark hair. "I lucked into some silly job in Austin, Texas, when internet stocks were going through the roof, and got out before the bottom fell out."

"What did you do for them?" she asked. "What was your job title?"

She wanted some sense of who the hell he was out in the real world. All she had was some gauzy memory of the quiet, high school poet-boy who'd seemed not of this world, somehow. Surely, that wasn't the real Nathan Booth.

"I don't think I even had one," he admitted. "I basically wrote music for videos they were making to sell the product they were peddling. It was silly. But the music-loving millionaire who founded the company liked me and gave me stock options and the whole nine yards. My restless soul spared me from the down side. I left just in time."

"Lucky you."

"Yeah. Lucky me. What about you, Jane? Did you finish college? Do you like managing the coffee shop?"

"No, and yes," she said. "Didn't even make it through the first year at Pitt. I just felt like there was nothing they were teaching me that I didn't already know, and I didn't feel like wasting my time. And, yes, I love managing the coffee shop. I love Pembrook. I'm not even sure why. Guess I'm just a simple, country girl."

"Remember that CSNY song, *Country Girl*? Off Déjà Vu?"

"Yeah," she said.

"I love that song."

"Me, too."

Neither one spoke right away. Jane turned so that she stood with her back to him and tried to gaze at the wall of trees that surrounded them. It occurred to her that she didn't know why she'd come, what she hoped to have happen or wanted to say. She felt him standing next to her then, their arms almost touching, but not quite.

"It's okay, Jane," he said softly, just above a whisper.

She turned and fell into him, as she had with Mike hours before. She was a serial breakdown artist – the heartbreak kid. Without quite knowing she was doing it, she lifted her face and looked at his, reached her hand behind his neck and forced his lips down to meet hers. Their mouths opened in a deep, easy kiss. They both tasted like coffee.

"I'm sorry," she said, after stepping back from their embrace. "I don't know what the hell I'm doing, Nathan."

"Well, whatever it is, it's okay."

She suddenly knew that she had to go; she simply couldn't be there one more instant. She headed for the jeep and said, "Forget this happened, Nathan. I shouldn't have come here."

"Jane," he called, but she was already pulling away.

Susan dispensed a soft, sticky line of whipped cream from its container onto Kenton's midsection – from the center of his chest to his navel, to be exact. "Hmmm," she said seriously. "Do I eat my way up, or down?"

"I'm thinking down."

"Feeling greedy are we?"

She did as he suggested, using her tongue to erase the fluffy white trail and then set about undoing the waist button of his jeans with her teeth. Kenton started laughing as the task proved more difficult than anticipated. Just as the button came loose, there was a knock at the door.

"Are we expecting company?" Susan asked as she jumped up.

Kenton refastened his jeans and also stood, as Susan went to the door. She pulled it open and Milo Lewis stood there beside a man Susan didn't know.

"Milo freaking Lewis," she said. "What the hell are you doing here?"

"Nice to see you, too, Susan," Milo said amiably. "This is Stan Markham. He's with Columbia Records."

"This is Kenton Hall," Susan replied, taking a step backward as the visitors entered. "He runs the Ghost Tree documentary."

Milo approached Kenton and extended his right hand, which Kenton shook. Stan Markham did the same.

"You have something on the tip of your nose," Milo said, looking back at Susan.

"It's my new thing," she said. "You like it? I was just about to eat some dessert actually." She wiped the white dot from the tip of her nose. She then picked up the easy-to-operate, hand-held camera Mandy left for them should they have any 'inspirations' and pointed it at the interlopers. "So really, Milo, what inspired you to make the trip?"

"I just wanted to tell you guys in person how much I love what I saw this morning. It's absolutely sensational. Really."

"Is there a 'but' coming?" She paced the room, pretending to be a visionary and highly artistic director.

"No," Milo said. "No, 'buts' at all. Really. I couldn't be happier. We'll have to make a few little technical improvements, but it won't have any effect on the content."

"Can you elaborate on that?" Kenton asked, pulling the chair from the desk and having a seat. Milo and Stanley sat on the edge of the bed that Susan and Kenton had just been preparing to utilize. Susan remained standing.

"Just enhancing the audio a bit, maybe tightening up some of the edits. Things that will only improve exactly what's there."

"Sounds reasonable. Don't you think that sounds reasonable, Kenton?"

"Yeah. Sounds reasonable."

Susan saw that Kenton's skepticism was slow to leave his eyes yet felt certain Milo meant them no harm. She pointed the camera directly at the bespectacled sidekick, who looked remarkably like Susan's twelfth grade physics teacher.

"So what are you doing here, Stan?" she asked.

Milo interjected, "I took the liberty of letting him see the video, and he was as blown away by the band as I am. We both feel like we're being given a chance to correct history, if I can be so bold. You know … it feels like destiny screwed up, the whole world should have heard those songs … and Nathan's voice … twenty years ago. We want to make it all right."

"So Columbia Records is prepared to offer a deal to Ghost Tree?" Kenton asked.

"Yes," Stan confirmed. "We are. I can't remember being so excited by a band. It reminds me of when I was a kid. I was trying to explain to Milo on the plane how all this stuff is reminding me of how I felt when I first got into this business. I would have walked barefoot for twenty miles to knock on some radio programmer's door, even though I knew it was a one in a million chance that they would play my band's song. But I believed in it, and that was what mattered. That's how I feel right now … and it's almost like the whole documentary you guys are making is about how as a culture we've kind of lost that feeling. And maybe it's time to correct that."

Susan was impressed. She had talked to many bullshitters in her day – most of them male, and many of them in the music business – and this guy seemed to be a little different.

"So let's be clear," Kenton said. "These guys, who haven't played together in twenty years, who are all over thirty-five and have established careers – and one of them, a family – are not only about to have their story told on national television, they're also about to be offered a deal by Columbia Records." Her lover's sizeable suspicion seemed to be morphing into amazement.

"Yep … that about sums it up," Milo said.

Stan added, "I thought maybe we could get them into a studio somewhere close and record one or two songs … or maybe more … so we might even be able to rush out a single at some point during the show's run."

"And when do you see the show beginning its run?" Susan asked.

"I actually have a team on promos now and was hoping to have this first episode on the air next Monday night."

"Are you fucking kidding me?" Kenton yelled. "That's seven days from now, man."

"That's how it works, guys. It's the time of the year when I have to get stuff out there in a hurry … and this feels like it might benefit from urgency on all of our parts. The story will unfold as we make it."

"I like it," Susan said, extending her arm and turning the camera on herself momentarily. "Let's just go with the flow here, Kenton. Whatever happens, it should make for some cool viewing. Now we better get our butts out to Berg's if we want to be sure to beat the band members to their twenty-year reunion."

Trey Rush was a lean, pale, mild-mannered man. Mandy had worked with him ten years before on a never-to-air series pilot for NBC, and the two had struck up a friendship. It was not uncommon for Mandy to call Trey to ask his opinion about a new piece of gear on the market, or to tell him about a particularly comical or disastrous shoot she'd survived.

"Hey, TR," she called as she strolled across the grassy parking area outside of Berg's barn. Trey's two assistants emerged also from the large, white Dodge van.

"Hey, Mandy," Trey said, accepting her quick embrace. "Thanks for the call."

"Thank you for making it out here on such short notice."

Trey introduced Mandy to Artie Puchka, whose considerable girth and weight made his entry into the day's sunlight seem like an eclipse in the making, and to Karla Stoudt, who was as thin as Artie was not. All three of the techies seemed to be on unfamiliar terms with sunlight, with pasty complexions and squinting eyes.

"Brought you a surprise," Trey announced as he led Mandy to the back of the van. He opened the doors revealing a state-of-the-art sound system in addition to the state-of-the-art video equipment Mandy had been expecting.

"Jesus, Trey. Who'd you rob to get all this stuff?"

"Called in some favors," he said. "From what you said on the phone, I thought this thing should sound as good as it looks."

The group set about unloading the van as Mandy told them the story of how she had landed 'the sweetest gig' of her career.

The May afternoon felt more like summer than spring. As Mike drove up Berg Lane he couldn't fight the feeling of déjà vu. He didn't even try to. The sunlight dappled the dirt road ahead of him and ushered him backwards in time. By the time he parked beside the large white van, he was eighteen again. He noticed Kenny Maxim and Jonathon Hilliard already inside the barn. They were both in the process of setting up exactly where they had always set up: Kenny's drums in the center toward the back, the circle's far border, and Jonathon to Kenny's left, next to Ron Berg's giant Hammond organ. Mike's sense of *déjà vu* deepened.

"Hey, Mike," Jonathon yelled as Mike lugged his amp and bass through the opened doors.

"Mike Collins," Kenny added, with a big grin.

"Jonathon, Kenny," Mike called back before laying down his burden and coming over to shake hands. "Hey, Sam," he added when he noticed Jonathon's oldest daughter seated on a hay bale. "Didn't know your dad was a rock star, did you?"

"No, not really," Sam said. "Although, he's been trying to tell me for years."

"He's been trying to tell everyone," Kenny added.

"Can you believe this is really happening?" Jonathon asked. "I mean, this is pretty wild isn't it, Mike?"

From Jonathon's tone, Mike could tell that the spry Admissions Dean had just made the same observation to Kenny. He'd probably been making the comment to anyone he'd encountered in the past few days.

"Yeah," Mike said. "It's pretty wild. And where'd we get all the nifty-looking equipment?" he asked, noticing the speakers placed around the barn's dusty, sunny, spacious interior.

"Right here," the short camera girl, Mandy, announced, holding the hand-held video camera that seemed attached to her permanently. "Actually, my friends from Pittsburgh brought it all."

It was then Mike realized there were others lurking in preparation: A thin girl running cable from a camera to a soundboard; a severely overweight man lifting a speaker onto a stand; a man on a ladder adjusting lights.

"Mandy, can you stand by Nathan's mic?" the ladder-man called down.

"Got ya, TR," Mandy replied. "Let's hope everything works," she added to Mike.

At that moment three more vehicles pulled up. Kenton, Susan, and two strangers emerged from one, Jane emerged from the second, and Nathan Booth emerged from the third.

"Looks like we have ourselves a rock and roll band," Kenny said, clearly happy with the prospect.

Mike returned to his station just to the right of Kenny and set about plugging in his amplifier and getting out his bass. A self-consciousness he recognized from his teen-aged years seemed to be accompanying the rush of memories. His instrument would serve now as it had then – as a barricade of sorts. As he strapped on his bass he wondered about the identities of the two men accompanying Susan and Kenton.

"Jane," he heard Jonathon and Kenny say in near-perfect unison, followed by a happily hollered "Nathan."

"Hey guys," Mike added, not wanting to be rude, and yet unable to feel connected to the moment. Nathan came over and extended his right hand. When Mike reciprocated, the singer pulled him into an awkward top-heavy embrace above Mike's bass.

"Father Michael," Jane said from across the room and added in a faint brogue, "top of the evening to ya."

Mike smiled on cue but quickly glanced away. For the next twenty minutes or so each of the band members remained focused on his or her set-up, the occasional spark of nervous conversation bouncing among them. Small talk.

The sun was setting by the time they were actually ready to make music. It was then, thankfully, that Mike's self-consciousness began to fade, as the band fell into the roles they had played all those years ago, the circle complete as Jane and Nathan took their posts. The perfect evening, the hovering strangers, the mysterious guests, the curious teenager and smiling-faced TV producers – all disappeared as the five old friends began to search for a song in exactly the same way they had twenty years before.

A chord progression became the glue that held them all, suspended just a few feet above the wooden barn floor. It seemed like a ballad at first, but as Kenny began to understand it better, it gathered momentum, became a bit more aggressive, anthem-like. Nathan's voice cut through. Words about dragonflies and water-wheels, sawdust and summertime peppered the air.

"Never thought that I could ever make it back again," was the line to which he seemed to keep returning, the mantra fighting for prominence within the music's messy poetry. "Never thought, never thought, never thought," and they all intuitively paused before resuming as he finished, "I could ever make it back again." And there it was: the first new Ghost Tree song in twenty years.

They lingered in their new creation for a good long time before segueing into *Mystic Light*, which felt new and familiar at the same time. Kenny smiled his mad, angelic smile, and Jonathon called something to his daughter who nodded with more love than Mike could ever remember seeing on any child's face. Nathan held his eyes closed, singing.

Just as the band instinctively rounded another bend, *Mystic Light* merging into another new reading of one of their old songs, Jane pulled her guitar over her head and set it down. Mike watched, assuming she was making an adjustment or taking a sip of her water, her actual intentions not registering.

"I can't do this," she said into her microphone and ran from the barn.

Rather than chasing after his friend, Mike did what he had done another lifetime ago. He watched her go away.

A fallen branch had made her seat in the woods uncomfortable, yet Edith hadn't moved or shifted. She had always preferred at least a small degree of discomfort. It was familiar to her. She twisted a strand of thin brown hair between her fingers as she peered through binoculars at the scene in the distance.

The softening blue sky bled darkness as the light from within the barn cast itself outward. The people there, the people Edith watched now, were all placed perfectly: a living, breathing, beautiful American painting. And the music only amplified the overall effect. Ghost Tree was everything Edith had known they would be, and more.

Before Edith actually saw the shift in the barn, she felt it, and so was not exactly surprised when Jane ran out to her car, got in and drove away. It almost felt to Edith as if it had been scripted. Everything was scripted, she thought – her whole life, a long, tedious script that only now was turning interesting.

Rather than run to the highway and jump in the wagon, she chose to remain where she was. Before long, the others emerged, figures standing in the near-darkness. She heard the vague rhythms of their parting conversations. One by one they got in line, a carnival caravan that convoyed slowly down the long dirt lane and back into reality. Edith sat hidden – the first song still playing in her head.

"My holiness blesses everything I see."

Nathan Booth whispered these words as he turned away from the line of cars. He glanced at the trees and road signs, the shrubs and houses, as he drove.

"My holiness blesses everything I see," he whispered again, farther now, closer to home, glancing at the sky, the stars, and the big, white moon. Nothing was beyond the scope of his murmured incantation.

"My holiness blesses everything I see," he said to his house, to his car, to his Fender guitar as he went around back to the stairs that led up to his rooftop station. From there, he looked down the mountain and saw the faint blip of light that was Pembrook. He thought about Jane and her pain and the band and the song that had fallen from heaven, or so it had seemed.

"My holiness blesses everything I see."

He had come here, come home, for this. He had come to kiss Jane this afternoon and to watch her break down tonight and run from the barn. He had come here to shake Mike's hand and to smile and play with Jonathon and Kenny. He had come here to build this house and stand on this balcony and have these thoughts. He had come here to look back across time only to discover that it, along with everything else, was pure illusion.

"My holiness blesses everything I see."

He whispered the words one last time before walking inside to sleep.

Stan Markham sat alone at the desk of his threadbare motel room. In a minute or two he'd join the others in Mandy's room where they were all busy reviewing the night's remarkable footage. Though Jane's abrupt departure was clearly fueled by pain, it would make for good viewing. No doubt about that one. But Stanley couldn't concern himself with that right now – he was still processing what he had heard out in that barn.

He remembered the day he first walked into the offices at A&M Records in New York, a nineteen-year-old Jewish kid from Pawling, humming Clash songs on the subway and plotting a revolution of sorts. He remembered when he'd been sent to Ireland to see the Alarm and how he'd broken down crying and then ran to call his boss as they finished their first song. He remembered the stadium in Dublin in which he'd seen U2 on the final night of the Joshua Tree tour, and how vividly it had reminded him that music has the power, literally, to move mountains. At least that was how it had felt to him then as he jumped up and down in the gentle spring rain with fifty thousand brothers and sisters.

Where had that gone? That world had simply disappeared for him. He guessed there were kids still being lit up by music, and yet, in this new age of portable entertainment and disposable everything, it all was sadly, tragically, different. Things were too easy, too manipulated. So they could never mean as much.

At least he felt that way until tonight. Maybe it was because the music of Ghost Tree was born at another time – the time that he now recalled so fondly – it took him there again. That first song, the one that nobody, not even the band, had ever heard before that moment, was what did it more than anything. As he witnessed their joyful discovery of something that had never been lost, something that time could not diminish, something upon which age, station and background had no bearing, he remembered the secret he'd forgotten – music was magic.

The face of the keyboard player's daughter smiled again in his memory, and he knew that she had known it, too. Right then, they were brother and sister, bouncing up and down to a song.

7

Pembrook was a ghost town Tuesday morning.

"Ghost Tree in a ghost town" Susan thought as she walked along Broad Street, the darkness only just beginning to recede. Her next thought was, "I'm hardly ever up this early. I like being up this early."

Though she'd barely slept, she felt awake and alive and very content. She smiled at each new storefront. "Maybe we'll live here one day," she thought.

She breathed deeply as her steps took her closer to her predawn destination: Steerbucks. She was hoping to gently ambush Jane Taylor. She had brought along the trusty hand-held camera, but knew a recorded interview was unlikely – and wasn't her primary objective. She really wanted to recruit Jane for the afternoon recording session they'd set up in Pittsburgh. Stan Markham had mentioned it to the rest of the band after the rehearsal's abrupt ending and they'd all been game. Only Jane was an unknown.

As if on cue the light inside the coffee shop went on as Susan entered her journey's last block. When she got to the window she peered inside and saw a short, young girl preparing the morning's initial batch of brew.

"Hello," she said to the solitary worker-girl who looked pale and uncertain, yet oddly beautiful.

"Hello?"

"My name is Susan Clawson. You can call me Susan, or Sue, if you'd prefer. Though nobody ever calls me that."

"Edith," the girl said, uncertainty still in her voice.

"Beautiful morning out there, huh? What special blends are you brewing up back there?"

"Jamaican Dark and the house blend, which is the same every day."

"Think I could get a big cup of the house blend?" Susan asked. Edith filled a to-go cup and handed it over. Susan took a sip. "I can almost feel my brain unlocking. I'm such an addict. Is your boss in?"

"She's in the back," Edith said. "Want me to get her for you?"

"Actually, Edith, would it be okay if I went back there?"

"I guess so," the girl said, with what Susan thought might be relief.

"Thanks, Edith." Susan set a five-dollar bill on the counter. "Keep the change."

At the back of the long, narrow, rectangular room she came to a door that held a sign that read 'Office' and knocked softly.

"Come on in, Edith," she heard Jane say, and temporarily played the part of Edith, gently pushing open the door.

"Jane?" she said as she eased her head into the small, cozy, dim-lit room, "it's me … Susan Clawson. Your trusty Ghost Tree stalker."

"Come on in, Susan." If Jane was surprised by the visit, her voice did not betray it. "What are you doing here?"

"I won't take too much of your time. I just wanted to make sure you were all right. Ooh – I'm liking the shag." Though the floor of the coffee shop was hardwood, the office, mysteriously, was covered with deep, red, shag carpet.

"The crazy owner's idea. He wanted a comfortable space to relax … of course, that was before he realized he would never actually come here."

"It is quite cozy. Makes me want to throw off my shoes."

"Be my guest."

"So … are you all right?"

"Yeah," Jane said, "I'm okay."

"You want to talk about it?"

"Not really."

"And there's that whole thing of you not really knowing me, too," Susan said. "Would it help if I confided that my favorite color is a shade of blue called periwinkle? And my favorite Beatle was George. Oh … and I'm a registered Independent."

Jane smiled then said, "I don't know what's going on with me. I can't seem to keep it together lately."

"Is it the music? Is it hitting you in some deep place or something?"

"Yeah … I think that's part of it. It's a bunch of stuff, Susan. I don't want to talk about it."

"I understand," Susan said. After a brief pause, she added, "I wanted to mention something that I'm hoping you'll be up for doing today."

"Already heard," Jane said. "Mike left me a message. The big recording session. Is Columbia Records really interested in Ghost Tree?"

"Yeah, I think they are. And do you want to hear something crazy? The Columbia exec who was at the rehearsal last night, actually seems like a pretty sincere and semi-decent human being. Can you believe it?"

"I'll do the session," Jane said. "On one condition."

"Name it."

"You promise not to try and 'open me up' in front of the whole world."

"Done," Susan said, though that was exactly what she planned to do eventually. "You need a lift down there?"

"No," Jane replied. "I'll go it alone. I still need to brush up on the old catalogue. Sounded pretty good last night though, didn't we?"

"Just a little," Susan said. "Guess we'll find out later if that was a fluke."

"I guess we will. As long as I don't go all Lifetime Movie on everybody again."

Susan laughed, and the women exchanged goodbyes.

"No whipped cream, please. And make the milk low fat. And not too hot, either, hon."

Andrea Weardon was Edith's most particular customer. And every day the details changed. One morning the recently retired dental hygienist might require every single fattening ingredient available, and the next one, like this one, she might be feeling more Spartan and forgo an abundance of earthly pleasures.

Edith handed over the drink with a smile. "Have a great day, Mrs. Weardon."

It was thanks to Jane that Edith had learned the majority of the customer's names. It was also thanks to Jane that Edith had learned to smile at people, occasionally even going so far as to look them in the eye. Jane was easily the most personable and friendly woman Edith had ever known. She tidied the counter, awaiting the next meek flurry of customers.

"You all right, Edith?" Old John asked, standing at the counter. "Think you got that spot," he chuckled.

Edith forced her arm still, embarrassed by the ferocity with which she now realized she'd been polishing. "Why do you ask?"

"You seem a little preoccupied is all. Sure didn't mean any offense."

"I'm sorry," she replied. "I'm actually doing pretty great, though." She turned away and set about pouring the old man his morning decaf.

"Just remember, things are never as good as they seem or as bad as they seem. They're always in the middle."

"I'll try to keep that in mind." Her right hand shook as she handed over the drink.

"Always," he said again, a look of concern on his face. "Every single time."

He walked away and Edith had the sudden urge to scream the word "fuck" at the top of her lungs. She wasn't sure why.

Jane attempted book-keeping in the office, as soft knocks interrupted her for the second time that morning. Again, she mistakenly assumed they belonged to Edith.

"Jonathon," she said, as the piano player opened the door.

"Hi, Jane. Hope I'm not disturbing you."

"Oh, I'm always a little disturbed, Jon."

He smiled his broad, pink-faced Scottish-American smile as he walked into the office. Jane sensed his discomfort. "You okay, Jon?" she asked.

"I should be asking you that."

"Oh, last night," she said. "I don't know what was up with me. Guess I kind of lost it."

"It's okay. I think we're all a little overwhelmed at the moment. I know I am." He swayed in place. "Jane, I want to apologize to you. It's occurring to me over the past few days that I've been harboring a resentment against you all these years, and I'm sorry for that."

"What are you talking about? If anyone should be apologizing it's me. I should never have left like I did back then."

"But that was twenty years ago," Jon said. "Twenty years. Two decades. And I'm sure you were only doing what you felt you had to do … whatever the reasons. I just wanted to tell you I'm sorry for holding on to that for so long and that I forgive you, if you feel like you need to be forgiven."

Jane couldn't manage a response.

"That's really all I wanted to say," he added. "Think we should hug or something?"

Jane broke out laughing and went to him. After he left, she turned to the mirror on the wall, and searched her eyes for the person she had been all those years ago. She thought she saw a spark of something. She sure hoped that it was courage.

"Damn, we were good."

Kenny Maxim made this observation as he drove his VW bus toward downtown Pittsburgh. Jonathon Hilliard was the lone recipient of his observation. Their musical gear was loaded compactly into the vehicle's deceptively spacious rear area. Jonathon drummed the dashboard, echoing the fill leading into the chorus of *She Took the Key*.

"So what did you think of rehearsal?" Jonathon asked.

"Do you mean the playing part, or the Jane walking out crying part?"

"The playing."

"Well the playing was pretty much like a dream … for me, anyway. It felt like no time had passed at all. I think it was actually the most bizarre experience of my life. When we started getting into that first song I felt like we all traveled through time. I was eighteen again, Jon. You know what I mean? It wasn't kind of like that, it *was* that. I was back there again. We all were. I'm still buzzing from it."

The blond-haired drummer shook his head for emphasis, switching his car back to the slow lane of Interstate 79.

"The crazy thing for me was the way my daughter reacted," Jon said. "She couldn't stop talking about it. I think she was even crying at one point during the rehearsal."

"Seriously?"

"She was moved, Kenny. And that's no small feat for a teenager. I didn't give a second thought to calling in sick today and heading off for this recording session. I feel like it's all bigger than us somehow."

"What about Jane, though? We need her."

"I talked to her this morning. She seemed okay."

Kenny remembered a scene from twenty years ago, one he had never shared with another living soul. In his mind's eye, he saw Jane Taylor in a neighborhood of Pittsburgh called Shady Side. It was seven months after Ghost Tree's last gig, and Kenny was there playing with his new band, Stinging Rain. As he was carrying the last of his kit into the night's venue, he saw Jane walking slowly in the distance – from a car, up some steps, then into an apartment building. But the most striking aspect of the sighting was not the coincidence of running into his old band mate so far away from Pembrook; it was the condition of the old friend.

Jane was pregnant – very, very pregnant.

Kenny never told a soul.

It was not yet noon and Mike was nearly finished drinking his second Michelob. He sat in a bar called 'Mickey's Big Mouth' in the neighborhood of Dormont, a few miles from downtown Pittsburgh. An elderly man sat two stools to his right, chain-smoking. He didn't talk much, but his steady wheezing was easily as loud as the country music being piped through the ceiling.

Mike had arrived at the Diocesan Building a little after nine that morning, having spent the entire night composing a letter to the Bishop. The letter outlined Mike's reasons for needing time away from the priesthood. He had made the mistake of calling Father Bill from the road, and the concerned friend had alerted the powers-that-be of Mike's pending arrival, making a quiet, unnoticed delivery impossible. Mike had been forced to speak at length with Father Slater, the Bishop's very intimidating right-hand man.

Drinking the last of the bottled beverage, he remembered their circular conversation, which always returned to the simple fact that Mike was unhappy and that, ultimately, his unhappiness was a disservice to his parishioners – one with which he could no longer live. By the third go-round Mike had stopped caring so much about Father Slater's opinion and stated his own doubts more emphatically.

"Is it a woman?" the stern clergyman had asked.

"Among other things," had been Mike's stammered response.

He winced with the memory and forced his mind onto different terrain.

He thought about Jane – about the pain he had seen in her eyes just before her early exit the night before. He wondered about its origin, and sifted once again through the section of the past he assumed held the key.

Something changed toward the end of that summer, something big. He had convinced himself it had to do with Jane's father and his overbearing vision for his daughter's life-course, but deep down he had feared, he still feared, that it sprang from something else, from someone else – namely, Nathan Booth. Mike had taken the coward's road, preferring ignorance to knowing.

Mike's mother replaced Jane in his thoughts.

"You've made me very, very proud," she had whispered in his ear as they embraced on the day he was ordained into the priesthood. "I love you, Michael."

How saddened would she be when she learned of his decision to step away from what they had both assumed was his vocation, his calling? He hoped he wouldn't break her heart, and ordered one more beer.

Milo had the TV set up in the studio lounge and was making sure it was set to play. He fiddled with some buttons and overheard Stan in the control room, talking microphones with the engineer, David Salem. Something about 'limiters,' he thought. Mandy and Kenton passed by, strategizing shots and camera-angles.

"Are they a couple of nervous Nellies, or what?" Susan asked with a smile, seated on the sofa just a few feet away. "Hey guys," she added, as Jonathon and Kenny walked in, lugging equipment. "You need some help?"

"Sure," Jon said. "I'm never one to turn down assistance."

Milo continued fiddling with the visual apparatus. He was actually attempting to attach his laptop to the television, and was finding the procedure less intuitive than he'd hoped. Suddenly the screen went blue and the letters 'AV' appeared at the top. He took this as a good sign. After he'd pressed his space bar and verified that he had, in fact, succeeded in achieving his goal, he joined Susan to help with the load-in.

Twenty minutes later, they were all there occupying every available seat in the small studio lounge. Nathan had been last to arrive, and sat on the floor with his long legs stretched out in front of him. Mandy, of course, was always in motion, recording at her odd, inspired angles.

"Sorry about last night everybody," Jane said by way of an icebreaker. "I don't know what got into me." Jon, seated to Jane's right on the sofa, patted her reassuringly on the back.

Milo instinctively liked Jane. What was it about her? Sure, there was her winning appearance. But beyond that she seemed sturdy ... trustworthy – like you could tell her your secrets. Not that he had any. He was too damn busy for secrets.

"Before we get into the recording," he began, "I wanted to show you all the rough cut of the first episode ... which will be airing next Monday, by the way." He responded to the gasps, "Holy shits" and "Oh my Gods" by saying, "I know it seems fast, but that's the way it works in my world. When something's right, you run with it. And this is right. And now is the time. I think when you see it, you'll know what I mean. I'd like to also mention that I'm thrilled that all of our paths are intersecting right now. I feel like a lucky observer."

"Save it for the Emmys," Susan yelled.

Milo smiled, and nodded for Stan to hit the lights. He'd seen the show a dozen times and focused now on the faces of the band members. This was crucial to the project's continued momentum, he thought. If they got excited about what they saw, they'd be that much likelier to cooperate in all the ways they might be asked to – the biggest item, of course, being their agreement to perform the concert that would serve as the series' climax.

His mind was put to ease almost immediately. Each face he studied looked child-like in its way. Which was exactly what he had hoped for. He hoped they, along with the rest of America, would be transported to a time when life was simpler.

Jane couldn't take her eyes from the screen. She kept her hand on Jon's forearm as if they were ascending a slow, steep rollercoaster hill that was setting them up for the terrifying yet thrilling drop. And though she knew the story, watching it this way made it all feel new, somehow. She even forgot the ending for the time being.

She loved each townsperson clip, from Mrs. Collins, to Old John, to Fay, to Larry Terk. What hit her hardest, though, was the rehearsal footage. They all looked so young and bright. And there was a kind of weightlessness surrounding them in the barn's filtered sunlight.

As the last frame disappeared, silence filled the room. Somebody turned the lights on. At that moment Jane really looked at Mike for the first time since his arrival. He looked like shit. She'd been so caught up in her own emotional struggle she hadn't considered that he might be in the midst of his own.

"That was amazing," Kenny Maxim said finally.

"Really great, guys," Jonathon added. "You actually managed to make us look slightly cool. No easy feat."

"Speak for yourself," Jane said. "And how awesome are Old John, and Fay, and everybody? I love that!"

"Me, too," Susan said. "Everybody shines."

When nobody spoke for another moment, the record company guy said, "Now it's my turn to talk." He looked more like a scientist than a music man. But Jane had learned never to judge books by their covers. "I know this is kind of crazy, but I feel like we're being given an opportunity here, and I'm hoping we can take hold of it. As Milo told you, I'm with Columbia Records and I'd like to offer you guys a deal. A record deal."

He gave the group a collective moment to process what he'd just said. Jane's first instinct was to jump up-and-down, and she wasn't sure why. Some kind of odd rock-and-roll dream gene perhaps.

"Did you just offer us a record deal?" Jonathon asked.

"Yes, Jon, I did. I want Ghost Tree to be on Columbia Records.

In fact, I'm not sure in all my time in the music business that I've ever wanted anything more. But let's not worry about that yet," the studio exec continued. "Lets just make some music here. Any idea what you guys feel like recording today?"

As the others began plotting, Jane stood and crossed the room to Mike.

"You okay, Mike?" she asked. "You're smelling a little Irish. Did you drink your breakfast this morning?"

"I'll survive," he answered cryptically.

Before she could ask what, pray tell, required surviving, she was summoned to her station.

Nathan lit the tall candle that sat on the wooden stool, and set his notebook on the music stand. His amp was in a different room, but rang through his headphones as he started to play. Gradually he heard everything else as well: Jane's guitar and voice, Mike's bass, Jonathon's piano then organ, Kenny's drums.

He closed his eyes. He always closed his eyes. Even back then, that had been his way. He saw so much more when his eyes were closed. Opened, they took in the usual things, people and objects and seeming points of interest. Closed, though – well, closed took him to a whole other world.

He was in that other world as it began to take shape. Something with a similar feel to what they'd started with last night – though this time they were quicker to get more aggressive with it. His voice was a bird in a strong wind. He saw himself turning to fly with it, with it, with it now. He was speeding along, higher than he'd ever flown – the clouds small below him.

"Never thought, never thought, never thought I'd get back there again."

That was the mantra, similar to the night before and yet different. Nathan barely even heard the words as he sang them. He was lost in his visions. He saw his grandmother waiting on the front porch, the loving destination of each Sunday afternoon adventure. He felt that embrace, her embrace, as it had been then, every time, erasing all the awkward silences, every looming secret that surrounded them there in their so-called home.

"You run like the wind," she would say each time, tousling his hair with her small, rough hands. *"You run like the wind."*

And now here he flew, a child again, a child-bird soaring through time and space, an angel, a spirit, a freed captive of the ancient ghost tree. Here he was, his voice an invisible road through the sky.

Was he singing those words or just seeing them, poems in clouds painted white on the endless blue sky?

And now he saw Texas the day he was born, the day he turned thirty and had his final shot of whiskey. The day he knelt on dirt and stretched his arms out like tree limbs and saw stars start to dance overhead and heard voices like whispers, only louder and louder, until he covered his ears, crying with absolute rapture – finally seeing through.

The front wheel touched down, an airplane on pavement, bouncing its way to steadiness as the song narrowed back down to earth and he finally opened his eyes.

Jonathon was the first band member to enter the control room. "My name's Jon," he said as he extended his hand to the engineer.

"David Salem," the bald, smiling, bespectacled man behind the controls said. "That was amazing."

One by one the others entered and Jon beamed at each one. He was dizzy with the whirlwind his life seemed to be, all of the sudden. Yesterday he had been the Dean of Admissions at Harrison College, and today he was a national recording artist.

"Way to go guys," he said to his comrades.

"You too, Jon," Mike said, patting the shorter man's back and taking a spot beside him.

"Damn," Jane yelled about two minutes into the playback. "We rule."

Stan Markham had taken a seat by David Salem and was listening intently.

"What do you think?" Jon asked.

"I think it's even better than it was last night. Look at my arm." He lifted it to display the army of goose bumps. "Where the hell have you people been all my life?"

Four minutes later, when the music stopped, he continued, "We can pare that down to the song I think it is."

"You mean we can cut all the goofing at the beginning and maybe some of the jamming in the middle and the end and make it a real song?" Kenny Maxim asked.

"Pretty much."

"Who knew?" Mike said.

Jonathon studied Nathan's face. As usual, the singer was the least talkative of the bunch.

"What did you think, Nathan?" he asked, emphasizing the "you."

"I just sing," came the soft reply. "You guys can figure out the rest. I trust you."

Jonathon's smile grew broader.

Edith and Molly ate dinner at Pembrook's lone Chinese restaurant. They were the only customers, and were mixing and matching from the dishes they'd ordered.

"I wonder what Dr. Kaufman does all summer?" Molly asked.

"I think he goes fishing down south somewhere. Some bayou in Louisiana or something like that."

"But how does he survive without conservative young Christians to torment for three months? I'm sure his cravings would stay strong. How would the beast stay fed?"

"He could always find some little old ladies to mess with. Maybe a befuddled clergyman?"

"True," Molly concurred. "Or maybe he calls into those prayer hotlines that you see bad-haired born-agains pushing on late night TV. I bet he could really rattle some cages there."

Edith was working hard at what she hoped would be considered normal-friend behavior. She sensed Molly's concern of late, and wanted to ease it. She concentrated with all her might on keeping her hand as steady as a surgeon's as she used her chopsticks to sample from each steaming plate.

"It feels good hanging out with you like this, Edith," Molly said. "I've been pretty worried about you lately. I was even thinking about calling your folks."

Edith shuddered at the thought of that telephone call, and the physical reaction tripped her out of the safety zone she'd been cultivating.

"Please promise me you won't ever do that," she insisted more aggressively than intended. "No matter what happens. Can you promise me that?"

"What does that mean?" Molly asked. "'No matter what happens.' What could happen?"

Edith felt unequal to the task of even beginning to explain to her friend all that might happen. The futility of their friendship and of the so-called normalcy she'd been seeking for so long suddenly shook free and stood there, clearly, for her to see.

Futility. Futility. Futility.

"I can't do this right now, Molly." Edith stood and pulled a ten-dollar bill from the front pocket of her jeans, as well as the keys to the Kring's car and set both on the cluttered table. "I need some air."

As she reached the door she called over her shoulder, "Don't you dare call my fucking parents."

It felt good to walk. She'd been cooped up in that car so much lately, it felt good to breathe the air and see the stars, which seemed to grow clearer and brighter as she moved away from town. And she liked the fact that she was laughing more than crying.

"Crazy people don't laugh at themselves," she observed aloud.

She knew where she was going, of course. She'd known from the moment she and Molly first decided to grab dinner. She could already hear the conversation she and Jane would have about everything.

"That's right," she said. "Jane will understand."

She would wait this out at Jane's house. And when Jane returned from her adventure in Pittsburgh, she would find her daughter sitting on the porch.

The band recorded a total of five songs, each one feeling better than the last. All but the first were from their original arsenal. Kenny Maxim's strong suspicion that he had entered some kind of time-space continuum persisted late into the night Tuesday. He was amazed at how little the music had aged. It somehow sounded even fresher now.

Jonathon would give voice to pretty much any thought that entered his mind regarding the wild Ghost Tree ride, but Kenny felt no such urge. He simply went through the experience and let his state of private awe blossom.

He had played enough mediocre music in enough mediocre bands over the years to know when something very un-mediocre was taking place … to know when a gift was being given. He decided not to sully the transaction with words, opting instead just to smile.

Kenton sat at the control panel with Susan beside him. For the tenth time in a row he reached over to the computer keyboard and

pressed the space bar. The last chorus of *Mystic Light* played and
—once again—a particular moment took his breath away.

"Do you need to be alone?" Susan asked, noting the near-sexual
reverie he seemed to have around this portion of the recording.

"Do you hear that? Or is it just me?"

"Of course I hear it you big doofus. It's fucking amazing." She
used her high-pitched Motown scream on the word "amazing."

"What have we stumbled into here, Susan?"

"Don't even ask, Kenton. Just smile … and maybe dance a little."

As she leaned toward him, the control room door opened and
Jane Taylor popped her head in.

"Think I could talk to you guys?" the pretty guitar player asked.

"On or off camera?"

"Believe it or not, on."

Mike pulled to the curb in front of Chet's old house – the house of
their childhood. A new family lived here now, but the look hadn't
changed: same wooden shutters, same red brick, same American
Beech tree swaying gently in the night.

Branches and sky.

It was after midnight. The street and all its houses were asleep.
He'd picked up a six-pack in Pittsburgh and was on the third can.
He sipped and stared, his mind numb.

How many nights had he driven here in his hand-me down junker,
the same junker that escorted Jane and himself to and from band rehearsals, and the three of them to dozens of movies and concerts and
late-night meals? A memory flashed of Chet laughing uncontrollably
in the back seat, milkshake spurting through both of his nostrils, only
escalating his hysterics, Jane and Mike laughing harder than he was.

Other memories came too:

The drive to Pittsburgh, following Jane the day after she'd gone;
the drive he had abandoned mid-way. The hours spent staring at
the phone, but never calling.

He feared her voice more than anything then, because through it his biggest fears might be validated. She just didn't think of him that way. She loved Nathan. Mike was only her friend. They all sounded so small and trivial now. But back then they had been boulders on his pathway.

Mike leaned right and opened the glove compartment. He dug out an old James Taylor CD he vaguely remembered living there, *Mudslide Slim and the Blue Horizon*. He hadn't listened to it in ages but threw it in, scanning to a song called *Riding on a Railroad*. There was something about the track, the plaintive-sounding vocals, the banjo, the flowing fiddle, the interweaving acoustic guitars – they all combined to provide him comfort.

He also thought he heard some advice in there from the honey-voiced journeyman. The lyrics resonated for Mike as they never had before – a chiming church bell in the dark night of his soul.

He sat listening – and eventually, smiling.

After spilling her guts on what would eventually be national television, Jane drove in silence. She didn't play the Ghost Tree disc she'd been listening to non-stop. She didn't turn on the radio, or even wind down the windows. She craved silence, and her craving was easily met. She was alone after all – making the same drive she'd made twenty years ago.

She felt something return to her. What was it, she wondered, as she rounded another bend on the monotonous interstate leading north from Pittsburgh? Was it the missing, third dimension to the two-dimensional façade she had maintained all these years? She had continued to play the part of the tough, free-thinking, unencumbered individual (with a capital 'I') but she'd been bluffing. But now, for the first time in forever, she felt like the bluffing was over. She was real again.

She pulled her car off the road and started to sob. But there was no sadness in her tears, none whatsoever. They were a river, leading her over falls she'd been avoiding since she was eighteen. The drop would be terrifying but somehow, she knew, the place where she landed would be so much more peaceful and satisfying than the place for which she'd been settling.

Feeling younger, stronger, she made the rest of the drive with the windows down and the music playing. As she pulled into her driveway close to two a.m., she noticed something amiss but couldn't place it at first. Then she realized what it was.

Edith Mathers was sound asleep on the floor of Jane's front porch.

8

"When I was a small boy, five years old or so, I would often go over to Joey Piros's house to play. Joey lived four doors over from us, and I'd walk through the intervening back yards to get from my house to his. One of our moms would watch to be sure I made it safely."

So began Mike's farewell homily that Sunday. He sensed the awareness beginning to form as a vague, apprehensive restlessness descended upon the worshippers.

"Late one adventuresome summer afternoon I noticed that neither mom was on lookout as I headed back home. There must have been a mix-up in communication. So rather than the direct route I always followed, I decided to take advantage of my momentary freedom to explore the forbidden forest that loomed behind the row of housing on our street. Now, this forest held every monster, every treasure, every dragon, every castle, every princess, every scary, magical, wonderful story I had ever been told. It was all in there, in the dark forbidden forest."

Mike noticed Jane sitting wide-eyed in the very last pew. He had avoided her concerned calls and visits by saying he was "sorting through some things" and assuring her that she'd understand better if she would swallow her agnostic pride and attend mass that Sunday. And there she was.

"I could never have articulated why I decided to go there then, into that place that scared me so terribly. Looking back now I think it had something to do with an impulse we all possess – an impulse to find ourselves, to face our fears, to see who we really are.

"I'm not one-hundred percent sure why I'm bringing it up now, but when I first sat down to prepare this homily, which I knew might be the most important of my life, or at least the one most remembered, this story popped into my mind. And when stories pop into my mind at homily-writing time, I am reluctant to dismiss them.

"I'm about to drop a bit of a bombshell on you. But first I want to say three things I know to be true with all of my heart. I know that God is love. I know I love all of you. And I know that in your trust and love for me, you have given me a gift I will never, ever, be able to repay. That said – I have decided to leave the priesthood.

"The decision is not taken lightly. I promise you. Many, many hours of prayer and reflection have led to it, and it is, hands down, the most difficult decision of my life. And yet, standing here this morning, I know it is the right one.

"When I joined the priesthood, I think I was clinging to that safe, well-traveled path from Joey's backyard to my own. I was avoiding the terrifying forest. Don't get me wrong – the backyard held some treasure. Every moment I've spent here with you, for example. I wouldn't trade a single one of them. Nor would I trade the privilege I've had of participating in some of your lives more deeply than I otherwise would have. What an honor it's been to share in your struggles and your triumphs.

"But it's time for me to brave the forest. For me that means joining you on that side of the pulpit and out there in the world. I wish I could say more about exactly where I'm heading, but the truth is I have no idea. I just know that I won't be going there as a priest. A dear friend of mine, Father William O'Shea, a far more capable priest than I ever was, will be taking over our mass schedule for the foreseeable future until my replacement is assigned."

Mike was suddenly overwhelmed with an almost unbearable heartache and was unsure if he could speak even one more word to these wonderful, caring people – his family.

"I was your friend before," he choked, "and I hope that I'll continue to be that now. Please remember that God loves you. And I do, too."

Somehow, miraculously, he made it through the remainder of the mass. An impromptu receiving line formed toward the rear of the church afterward and, to a person, Mike was wished well and addressed with compassion and kindness. Jane was the last in line.

"You okay?' she asked.

"Not really."

"Need a hug?"

"Yeah," he said. "I do."

The hug Jane gave him was the longest and most comforting of his entire life.

Susan Clawson had learned through the years that you couldn't force things. So just because she and Kenton envisioned this night – 'Debut Night' as they'd been calling it – as a major portion in episode three of the four part Ghost Tree series (Milo had already unearthed two other formerly broken-up small town bands to carry him through the remainder of the summer) didn't mean she could force a bunch of magic to take place. You couldn't manufacture stuff like that, not with real people involved. However, it was possible to help things along from time to time.

It was with this fact in mind that she invited Ghost Tree members to come to the Landmark Bar, to watch with their peers on the brand new seventy-two inch flat screen TV she had encouraged CBS to donate to the establishment. It was also with this in mind that she made sure the house sound system was upgraded for the night, and that all of The Allies' sound equipment, which she secretly hoped would be utilized by Ghost Tree before night's end, was piped directly into Mandy's most state-of-the-art camera and that Mike, Susan, Jonathon, and Kenny were all wired for sound. She intentionally left Nathan off this list because she liked leaving an air of mystery around him (not to mention the fact that he just didn't seem like a man who'd want his every conversation recorded.)

She had also been sure to invite key 'players' in the town such as Fay and Old John – in the hopes that others would follow. Susan soon realized that this last move was unnecessary, though. A tornado could not have kept people away from the Landmark Bar on the Monday night that part one of the Ghost Tree documentary debuted. Where else would people go to find the Super Bowl atmosphere they all clearly yearned for, surrounding this auspicious occasion?

Once she was sure that she'd done her part to set things in motion, Susan implemented another of her life's lessons – what will be, will be. It was out of her hands now. And as the room got crowded and the clamor escalated, she felt the familiar urge to get her suddenly empty hands on her man.

She spotted him talking with Mandy in a corner and, when she caught his eye, directed him, with a subtle nod, to their secret rendezvous point – the supply closet between the rest-rooms, which she'd commandeered for 'production headquarters.' When they were alone there she set about the task at hand. "Why can't I seem to stop wanting you?"

He moaned an answer, which she took to mean something along the lines of, "I have no idea, but I'm not going to question my good fortune because my dream lover Susan Clawson has taught me never to question my good fortune, and I always do exactly what that wise, beautiful woman tells me."

Mike felt as if there were a bubble of good will surrounding him. Of course, a trio of sixteen ounce Budweisers (courtesy of bartender Pete) and two shots of Jack Daniels (courtesy of God knew who) added to this sense, and helped Mike forget that his every word was being recorded. He sat with Jane at the bar, Larry Terk to Mike's right and Jonathon Hilliard to Jane's left. The hovering masses swarmed behind them, in anticipation of the show, which would begin in exactly forty-three minutes. Mike felt happy in a way that he hadn't in years. The freedom that came with yesterday morning's homily had the feel of longevity to it.

"What's the annoyingly unconcealed smile all about?" Jane yelled above the din.

"I don't know," Mike said, feeling the poetic swelling in his chest that often accompanied his consumption of more than a single beer. "I choose not to dissect it."

"That's a first."

"How's it feel?" Larry Terk asked, his chronic slur forcing more volume than his thin voice was used to. "Get yourself any poontang yet? If I left the priesthood, that would be the first thing I'd do."

Larry had apparently appointed himself ambassador for all red-blooded, blue-collared men, men who used words like 'poontang' indiscriminately and with great confidence, welcoming a lost sheep back into the fold. And in this moment he was, of course, overlooking the fact that he wasn't a priest, and also the fact the he and poontang were not exactly on familiar terms. Mike laughed.

"No, Larry ... thought I'd give myself a minute before jumping back into the game ... if you know what I'm saying."

"So what's the smile for, mister smiley smile?" Jane asked, laughing herself now.

"Didn't I answer that already? Oh wait, I guess I didn't. I'm happy."

"Thanks for clearing that up for us all."

Larry nodded his agreement.

"Would you say we're in the bosom of Pembrook right now?" Mike asked.

"You mean in the Landmark tonight?" Jane said.

"Yeah."

"I'm thinking it's more of an armpit type situation."

"Left ear," Larry offered definitively. "And the Brass Rail over near Mercer is the right ear."

Apparently Larry had given the matter some serious thought.

"I wish my daughter were here," Jonathon offered without segue or apology. "You know Sam, right, Jane?"

"Of course I know Sam. She's a sweetheart."

"She's really been affected by all this Ghost Tree stuff. I think she's as big a fan of our music as I am. It's really kind of bringing us closer together."

"That's awesome," Jane said.

Mike nodded, sipping the dregs of bottle number three.

"I kissed Nathan the other day." Jane leaned toward Mike in such a way that the words went to his ears and no one else's."

By some trick of grace Mike was not upset by the revelation – though, again, the alcohol may have played a part in his reaction. Whatever the cause, he felt no instinct to scream or bang his head down on the bar or anything along those lines.

"Did he kiss you back?" Mike asked.

"That's open to interpretation, I suppose."

"Was it everything you thought it would be?"

"Not so much," she replied.

Kenton had never been this guy. He had never been the guy getting laid in the back room; the guy who won the heart and body of the insanely beautiful girl; the guy the forces of fate tripped over themselves to help. And yet, here he was – that guy.

He sipped his whiskey and coke in the back corner of the bar and looked around at the sea of flannel and Red Man hats – 'his people' as Susan liked to call them. He had come full circle indeed. From Pembrook to Los Angeles to New York and back again – chasing his dream right back to the starting line. He always knew there was a story waiting here for him. And now, here it was, playing out on national television.

A hush fell as the room went dark and the show's opening image, the road into Pembrook, appeared on the brand new giant screen.

Kenton had watched his work with live audiences in other settings but none as pure as this one. If what these people saw did not ring true, they would surely make it known. And they wouldn't be gentle about it, either.

But the pain that usually came with this kind of shared viewing never materialized. In fact, just the opposite occurred. Kenton was completely relaxed as he watched. Within five minutes he knew that he had absolutely nothing to fear. He was safe.

At the first commercial break, Larry Terk, who had gotten a few moments of airtime, made a slow, drunken production of carefully climbing atop his barstool and bowing dramatically as people cheered for him. Later in the broadcast, Kenton noticed several audience members crying as interviewees remembered Chet Howard. Best of all, the whole room grooved and rocked as Ghost Tree of twenty years ago played their songs in Ron Berg's ageless barn. Kenton grooved and rocked right along with them.

He contemplated what it meant to be from a small town like Pembrook. You were always who you'd always been, he thought. He would forever be the shy, smart one. The kid who would one day grow up and hide behind a camera as he brought his stories to life. Mike was the cool, older kid who did the right thing, didn't curse much, and treated everyone with kindness, even little shy guys like him. Jane was the beautiful tomboy who was funny and independent, proudly walking along her solitary path. And they weren't stereotypes, he decided, they were identities. And yet, as the camera pulled away just a little more, the individuals faded into something else – a small, American town, where people took care of one another.

"Is this amazing or what?" Susan asked, moving in sync with him, reaching her arms around his waist. "I love these people."

"I love you," he screamed, with joy too big for his fragile heart.

About three quarters of the way through the show, Jonathon realized that in spite of how enthralled he was by what he was seeing and by the whole crazy Landmark scene, there was something missing. He'd started this journey with Samantha at his side, or at least it felt like he had; she should be with him now. He found Susan swaying with Kenton toward the back of the room and explained that he had to leave for a little while but would be back soon.

Moments later he pulled out of the packed parking lot and onto the quiet country road that led into town. Without thinking much about it, he turned on the radio. It was set to the only rock station in the area he could tolerate, WYKO in nearby Youngstown, Ohio.

"That's right," he heard the excited DJ say, "the band is called Ghost Tree, and they're from just up the road in little old Pembrook, Pennsylvania. Up until a week ago they hadn't played together in twenty years, but they were on national television tonight and I'm about to play a song of theirs that they just recorded. It's called *She Took the Key* and, as you'll soon hear for yourselves, it's pretty awesome. Only in America."

Jonathon nearly had a heart attack as the first harsh strains of Ghost Tree's most rocking song blasted out of his car speakers. It sounded amazing.

"Oh my God," he screamed to no one, pounding the steering wheel as his foot got heavier on the gas pedal. "Oh my God," he screamed again, wiggling in the seat, needing to move, to dance, to run.

He couldn't get home fast enough.

"Hey everybody," he yelled as he barreled through the front door. "We were just on the radio."

"You were just on national television," his wife, Carol, who could have been his twin with her wiry frame and short red hair, said. "What's so big about the radio?"

"I knew I'd be on TV tonight, but wasn't expecting the radio. I turned it on in the car, and the DJ was talking about us. This is all like a crazy dream or something."

Samantha ran into the hallway where the joyful meeting was taking place.

"Get a room guys," the beaming girl joked as Jonathon pulled his wife into him for a strong dance embrace.

"Can I take Sam to the bar?" he asked. "I think we're going to play tonight, and I want at least one of you guys to see it … to witness it."

"Sure," Carol replied. "I guess. Is that legal?"

"As long as I'm with her. And I think all bets are off tonight at the Landmark. It's a madhouse out there. People are going crazy for this stuff, Carol. We need to talk later. I don't know what the heck any of this means."

"We can talk all night, Jon. I promise. Now get back out there, and be the rock star you were born to be."

He ushered his daughter to the running car, thinking all the while about what an awesome wife he had.

Edith was back in driving mode. She'd been driving for hours. She listened to talk radio on an AM station and played her night at Jane's house over and over in her head. Her kind (if slightly surprised) boss had nudged her awake on the chilly front porch and guided her inside. She'd gotten pillows and blankets and made sure Edith was comfortable on the daybed. In short, she had mothered her.

"We'll talk in the morning," Jane had whispered as she brushed a hair away from Edith's eye.

And talk they had – bright and early, hours later, each surprisingly awake as they sat in Jane's kitchen together before leaving for work. Edith had felt comfortable, though not to the point of baring her soul or anything crazy like that. She was just happy to be there with Jane and Blue, the dog.

"I've been a little worried about you, Edith," Jane had said over glasses of orange juice. "You seem a bit agitated, if that's the right word. Finding you asleep on my porch last night didn't exactly ease my fears. Anything you need to talk about?"

"Nothing big, Jane," Edith had lied, fidgeting in her seat. "I'm just quiet by nature, I guess. And I was wondering how the recording session went so I came out and waited. Guess I must have fallen to sleep."

"I suppose I can buy that," Jane had replied. "And I'm kind of quiet too, sometimes – so I won't make a big deal out of it."

And now Edith drove. She had just watched the first Ghost Tree episode in the secret hideaway she'd made for herself in the lobby of one of the college cafeterias, the one nobody seemed to use all summer. There was a sofa there, which she'd nap on from time to time (when she wasn't pretending to sleep at the Krings', so Molly would stop her incessant fucking staring,) and an old Magnavox upon which she just watched the show.

"Just be sure and come find me if you need to talk," Jane had said on their three minute drive to the coffee shop that morning.

And that was exactly what Edith was doing right now – going to find Jane. She needed to talk.

Milo Lewis and Stan Markham were back in New York city – seated across from each other in a booth at Molly Malone's, the Irish pub located conveniently at the halfway point between their respective Manhattan office buildings. They had just watched the debut of 'Ghost Tree' amidst a crowd of strangers, the truest tell of all.

"I attribute it all to my lucky socks," Milo pronounced as he lifted a leg and revealed the weathered brown garment. "I was wearing these the morning I got my first job offer."

"You don't say," Stan answered dryly.

The friends were nearly finished with the single celebratory drink they'd allowed themselves. They were thrilled, to say the least, by what they had just witnessed, both on the screen and in the bar. The attention of the diners and drinkers had gradually shifted from private conversations to the television screens placed randomly throughout the establishment. And though Milo wouldn't have the numbers until the morning, he would have bet his life savings that the show was a hit.

"I'll be up all night working this thing," Stan explained.

"And you're sure the little handwritten deal you all signed in Pittsburgh last week is a binding legal document?"

"Absolutely," Stan said and then proceeded to fill Milo in on the radio war he'd been waging all week. So far, he had managed to get *She Took the Key,* his favorite Ghost Tree song and the first 'single,' to all of his targets, and each and every one of them had added it to their play lists. Normally, it took weeks, or even months of laying groundwork to get that kind of action, but the passion of the label exec and the ready-made story around the band, made it a pretty easy sell.

"Tonight I'll start to hit Europe and beyond. It's amazing what you can do these days with a song, a story, and a computer."

"Amen," Milo replied, raising the icy remnants of his drink for one final toast. "To Ghost Tree," he said.

"To Ghost Tree," Stan repeated.

The smiling, middle-aged men clinked their glasses and went their separate ways.

The Landmark was a zoo. No, it was a jungle. It had been a zoo before the show aired, but the animals had all been set free and now it was a jungle.

Mandy felt secure in the knowledge that she and Trey Rush had set up a dozen cameras all over the bar including the most expensive one she had ever seen, which was connected directly to the house sound system. There was no way they would miss anything important ... or even unimportant.

And somehow, Mandy knew, the band would be playing tonight. It was inevitable. There was already a murmuring rumor circulating, and she could feel it gathering steam. When Jonathon and his teenaged daughter entered and were instantly mobbed, it was clear that something had to give.

A voice broke through above the general chaos. Mandy looked to the small, cluttered stage and saw Susan Clawson's face beaming above all the rest.

"Hey everybody," Susan yelled. "How are you guys doing tonight?"

The place erupted in a unified, unintelligible, yet vaguely affirmative growl.

"That's what I like to hear. We just wanted to say how much we appreciate you all being here to watch the show. There will be three more episodes airing each of the next three Mondays. I say we meet back here for every one."

Another deafening roar.

"I was thinking how cool it would be if we could maybe get the band up here to play a song or two. What would you all think about that?"

The roar escalated, the throng, clearly, wildly in favor of the idea.

"Ghost Tree, Ghost Tree."

The chant started somewhere toward the rear of the room and worked its way forward. Susan started laughing at the microphone, then joined in. Kenny Maxim jumped up first and walked back behind his simple kit. Jonathon went next, grinning widely as he took a seat behind the borrowed keyboard. Jane and Mike followed, the crowd noise growing louder still. It was as if Led Zeppelin had surprised the group with an impromptu visit.

Mandy found herself smiling and nodding and cheering with the rest of them. She scanned the crowd for Nathan Booth and screamed like a schoolgirl when she finally caught sight of him making his way to the stage.

"There he is," she said excitedly to Trey. "Nathan's walking to the stage."

Nathan smiled at the crowd, picked up the only remaining available electric guitar and stood center stage.

"Hey," he mumbled into the microphone as he started making noise on the strings.

Nathan turned away from the audience and leaned, along with the other standing band members, towards Kenny Maxim. When they returned from their powwow they started into the new song, *Never Thought*.

Mandy knew all the words, at least as Nathan had sung them at the first recording session. Hell, she probably knew their songs better than they did. Though she had a feeling they didn't view songs the way most other people did. For most people, songs were solid objects, somewhat durable and consistent. But for them songs were something moving, liquid or gas, sunshine or moonlight. Yet, they seemed to be presenting this brand new one, at least generally, in the way it was recorded the week before.

Mandy could not have explained to Trey, or to anyone for that matter, why she was moved to tears then. But she was. Big bright tears that filled her eyes and traveled down her still-smiling face. It reminded her of the way she had felt when her best friend in college had taken her to a Baptist church, and the preacher had preached in a way that was so foreign and yet so exciting to her. She'd been caught up in the moment, eventually standing and dancing and testifying with most others in the church that morning. She testified now, raising both arms in the air, her whole body filled with a sense of expanding joy. She was a child in the rain. She was a girl on a beach with a soaring kite. She was alive with this beautiful music, which she had come to know like the back of her hand, like her own beating heart.

Casting her eyes through the crowd she saw that they felt it, too. This was not a college crowd by any means, and yet, for the moment, they'd become one. All of these hard-edged, hyper-real, working class people, became young, beautiful deadhead boys and girls swaying to the mysterious math of the music that only they knew how to calculate.

She saw Fay standing with her back to the bar, her right hand resting on her chest just above her enormous left breast – as if she were pledging allegiance. Which, based on the rapturous look on her face, was exactly what she was doing. She saw Jon's daughter, Samantha, dancing wildly, without a shred of self-consciousness, her brown hair flying and her thin arms flailing. She saw the head of the crowd's tallest man, a burly, bearded, flannel-wearing gentleman she'd noticed earlier. He started jumping up and down in the center of the room as the song picked up its final layer of intensity. She saw first his immediate neighbors and then the rest of the people joining him in the up-and-down dance.

"This is insane," she screamed to no one, though Trey moved closer and replied.

"I'm about to do something crazy," he yelled.

"What?"

"I'm about to do something crazy."

"What?"

He moved in front of her, blocking her view of the stage, and leaned down to kiss her hard on her lips. Mandy kissed him back.

If Jane were religious, she'd call it a miracle – the way she felt on the stage with these long lost friends, twenty million minutes evaporating into thin air behind them.

"Holy shit," she thought, then thought it again, smiling at Mike as the band navigated a surprise turn in *Mystic Light*, a bridge that hadn't been there before. The bar looked like a Bon Jovi concert video, especially during this, the lone ballad of the set. Lighters waved rhythmically in the air, bodies pushed closer into a single swaying mass.

She knew the weeks ahead would be difficult but, right then, nothing scared her. It was all okay. Jane had faith in her town and its people. Tonight, at least, she had faith in humanity at large and trusted it, finally, with her secret, which had lost all its power with the telling - which Susan had warned would air at the conclusion of the next week's episode.

She smiled again at Mike and he smiled back. She was a little tipsy and started to move with the song as they ripped right into *She Took the Key,* which Jon had just informed them he'd heard in his car on the radio.

They were on the radio. They were television stars.

"A roller coaster ride," she thought as she danced and kept looking at her best friend a few feet over on the stage. "This life is a wonderful roller coaster ride."

She'd been lucky. There was one spot open at the very back corner of the Landmark's gravel parking lot. Edith backed into it. She wasn't positive Jane was there, but thought it was a good bet. It seemed most of the town was here. And she thought she heard music, live music, coming from within. Was it Ghost Tree?

She wished she could unlock her forehead and just let it all fall out. She wished she could stop thinking and feeling so much all the time. She wished she could sleep and talk and live like normal people, or, at least, like she imagined they did. She yanked her hair, trying to enlarge her head, to make room for everything.

People started leaving the bar, in pairs and in groups, a few by themselves. There was laughter and loud conversation, and the fun they had all been having still clung to them. Edith stared from the darkness at the sauntering, disjointed group.

Wave one held no Jane. Wave two, the same. But still, she waited.

Though, technically, Nathan Booth was now fatherless, he still considered himself the prodigal son, returning home. He was grateful for the peace of the truck and the countryside and allowed himself a rare look backwards as he drove. He remembered the pivotal night he spent in Jackson Hole, Wyoming.

He'd sat alone at a ski-lodge bar, drinking himself into a slow, deep stupor. At some point, a woman sat down next to him, an employee, moving instantly at shift's end from server to servee. There were many empty places at the bar, but the stool beside his was the one that she'd chosen.

When Nathan drank, which had been getting more and more often, back then, he came closest to being conversational, and the off-duty waitress became the unwitting benefactor of his small window of articulation.

"How's it feel?" he had asked.

"How's what feel?"

"On this side of the bar."

"Same as it does every night," she'd answered evenly, close enough to him that he could smell the smoke in her hair even as they sat in the smoky room that had caused it. When she'd looked at him directly, her serious brown eyes sobered him momentarily, but only just. He'd seen something in them he hadn't expected: peace.

Many things had contributed to Nathan's estrangement from that particular state of being: a pathologically distant and unloving set of parents and their wordless departure from the world, a surprisingly violent and bloody stint in the military, a bitter break up, shortly after his discharge, with the only woman he had ever come close to loving.

"It's not so bad," the waitress had said to him that lonely winter's night. "Whatever it is, it's not so bad. In fact, it's not even real."

"It's not even real." That idea had stayed with Nathan. Like a pestering fly, it buzzed near his consciousness day and night and, though he hadn't known it at the time, his course had been altered.

To all appearances, he remained the same moping introvert, but a dim light came on and grew stronger each day. So that by the time he found the book, six months later in a quaint, cluttered shop clear across the country in Aston, Pennsylvania, he was ready for it. He read the words of the introduction and knew he had found the path, his path.

Within weeks, he had moved to the town in California that housed an institute devoted to the book and its concepts, and became a full time student. For years he did nothing but study, under the guidance, primarily, of one incredible, quiet, humble, and disciplined man.

He would be there still if he hadn't heard a voice, clear as his own, telling him he needed to go to Pembrook, to face his childhood, to help those who needed him there. And here he was. Driving through the night, almost home.

The largest office at Columbia Records was dark except for the square bright light of a desktop computer. Stan Markham was monitoring the hits on Ghost Tree's new MySpace page. One million and counting. It was truly amazing.

He had just made two calls to Australia. First, to a very powerful radio promoter there who had a line on a dozen of the most influential stations in all the major cities, and next, to a Columbia representative stationed in Sydney who'd agreed to follow up with the radio stuff and have all the retail chains ready for product the instant Stanley could get it there.

It felt good – like the old days.

Some people would argue that these tactics were obsolete, and yet they seemed oddly fitting where Ghost Tree was concerned. They'd cover the digital front, of course, but it felt good returning to the brick-and-mortar world. Stan's mission, he had decided, was to remind the world of a time when music felt real and essential, and of how a song could change your life if you let it. The music world had grown more and more superficial. Ghost Tree was the band to take things deeper again.

Within the next forty-eight hours he would have hundreds of conversations with hundreds of radio, marketing, and promotions people all around the world. His objective was simple: save the dying beast that was rock and roll.

The Landmark was emptying. Other than the suddenly chummy Mandy and Trey, Mike and Jane, and Larry, of course, Susan and Kenton were the last of the Monday night partiers.

"Forrest Tucker," Susan blurted to Kenton as they nursed their final drinks.

"Forrest Tucker," Kenton replied.

"Do you know who he is?"

"Of course," he said. "Star of the terrible yet lovable show *F-Troop*, from the mid-60s, I think it was."

"He was also in a great movie with John Wayne called *Chisum*," Susan added. "I loved that movie when I was a little kid."

After a pause, Kenton asked, "Any reason you mention Forrest now?"

"I just thought of him this morning for some reason, and it made me a little sad. He was obscure even in his own time and yet a million people knew his face."

"Yeah?"

"And now he's fading from all backward sight," she said. "He's like a road sign with the letters all gone. I guess I'm just sad that I know who Forrest Tucker is, but almost nobody else does any more, and nobody else ever will again."

"I think I get what you're saying, though it seems a little unlike you to be melancholy over time passing."

"I think that's why this whole thing feels so good, Kenton. It feels like we can show people an earlier time, to remind them of something that might be worth holding on to."

"What do you mean?" he asked. "What specific thing is it you want people to reach back for?"

"Innocence?" She paused, lost in thought. "Or maybe we're not getting further from anything. We're just people being people, same as ever."

"So you've already jumped to the other side of the fence?"

"Yeah," she said. "That's a woman's prerogative. Women can

change their minds, right, Larry?" she called to the man she'd never seen anywhere other than on that exact bar stool. She wondered if he had a hollow leg, literally. Surely the man had to urinate once in a while with all that beer and whiskey he consumed.

"Hell yeah," he said, his drunken glance sending a shiver through Susan who saw more leer than wry smile there in the bar's unforgiving closing-time light. Maybe being a lonesome alcoholic wasn't teeming with as much small-town charm as she'd initially imagined.

From the corner of her eye she noticed Mike and Jane making their way to the door, engrossed in conversation. She and Kenton continued theirs. They mapped out their plans for the next few days. First priority was setting a date and location for an official reunion concert, which would serve as the series' culmination. They'd talked to the band and met no resistance. Susan would also help coordinate continuing recording sessions. Stan Markham felt that with a few more days in the studio, they'd have something ready to release.

"Shit," Susan said, standing quickly. "I forgot to get Jane and Mike's microphone packs."

Was she angling for a scoop? Was she hoping to catch them making out in the parking lot? Was that why she had been sure to carry her trusty hand-held with her and why she had instantly put it to use once she was outside? She would ask herself these questions later, and be unable to answer definitively.

Whatever the case, the scoop she received was quite a bit bigger than anything she might have been hoping for – consciously or otherwise.

The parking lot was nearly empty. Jane and Mike walked through it at a leisurely pace.

"Can you believe this weather?" she asked.

"Jane," he started, suddenly filled with more words than he could speak, more feeling than he could hold. He stopped their walking. They stood facing each other and he forced himself to hold her eyes with his. Unwavering. "I need to tell you how sorry I am that I didn't stop you back then. Some weak part of me was even glad you were leaving, so that I wouldn't have to watch you falling in love with Nathan." He paused, fighting tears. "You were hurting, and I didn't try to help you. I'm so sorry for that."

"Mike, I'm not sure how to say this other than to just say it, but … I was … "

Before she could finish, Jane's name was called from two directions. Mike looked one way and saw Susan Clawson standing at the top of the Landmark steps calling to both of them. The other voice called only Jane's name and seemed to trump Susan's. All three of them looked into the dark half of the parking lot from which Edith Mathers slowly emerged.

"Edith?" Jane asked. "Are you okay?"

"You said … if I needed to talk … to come find you."

In that instant, Mike knew that this was a girl in trouble, standing on a precipice of some sort, one she'd most likely created herself. Mike knew that Jane, too, sensed the gravity of Edith's need.

"Yes," Jane replied. "That's what I said. I'm glad you found me."

"I have a secret," Edith said.

It was like they were all frozen. Mike felt an urge to yell something, to keep the girl from saying anything more while he and Susan watched. He thought Jane, alone, should hear the girl's secret, not him, not Susan. And yet, he simply couldn't bring himself to speak.

"I'm your daughter, Jane," Edith said. "I'm your daughter."

9

A week later, the same exuberant crowd flocked to the Landmark. And though this week the members of Ghost Tree were not in attendance, the same festive atmosphere reigned – right up through the portion of the show that documented the band's first recording session in Pittsburgh.

Kenton stood in the back of the room bracing for the change he knew was coming as the final segment aired. It featured the interview Jane Taylor had given them in Pittsburgh, the one that changed everything.

The murmuring of the bar crowd faded to silence as it became clear that something charged and personal was being revealed. There, on national television, Jane shared her twenty-year old memories of the final Ghost Tree rehearsal.

Susan: So Mike left early?

Jane: Yeah. He had a fishing trip or something the next morning. He was always my ride. But not that night. That one night I biked. *(She pauses, sipping some water.)* There's a path that leads down to the main road. It was all rocky and treacherous, especially in the dark – so I walked the bike for that part. Halfway down, I thought I heard something. I stopped and waited, decided it was nothing. It was totally dark. I started to feel scared and wasn't even sure why. *(She*

pauses again, and takes another drink of water.) I was almost
to the road when an arm reached out and yanked me backwards. I never saw a face. Never heard a voice. I only know
that he was stronger than I was, and that I couldn't break
free. He forced me face down onto the ground. I could
taste blood and dirt on my lips. I remember noticing that,
the blood and the dirt, the way they tasted together ... as
the bastard raped me.

The segment ended. It was a good minute before anyone in the
Landmark spoke and even then it was in whispers. Kenton watched
as people he had known all his life began processing their new view
of the world in which they lived.

Bright and early Tuesday morning, Jane stepped out of her house
with a smile on her face. As she got in her car, she scanned through
highlights of the eight days that had passed since Edith's parking-
lot confession.

Jane had taken Edith home from the Landmark that night, and
led her immediately to the guest room, sensing that the girl needed
rest above all else.

"Do you hate me?" Edith had asked as she settled in beneath the
daybed sheets.

"Why would I hate you?"

"Because I didn't tell you the truth."

In the ensuing conversation, Jane learned that Edith had discovered her true lineage in a hidden strong-box a year before, and had
chosen Harrison College because it was located in Jane's hometown. She also confessed that she had remained in Pembrook that
summer for the sole purpose of getting to know her birth-mother.

"Edith, look at me."

Edith's gray eyes had seemed to fight their way through groggi-
ness before settling on Jane's.

"I don't hate you. Not even a tiny little bit. I'm so glad you found me. I guess deep down I always hoped you would do this ... that one day a girl would show up at my doorstep and introduce herself ... now here you are. Please, please, know that this is a completely welcome surprise. I can't even tell you how hard it was letting go of you back then, even though I knew it was the right thing to do."

Jane had gone on to express her concern about Edith's emotional state, and gradually pried the girl's history out of her.

"First order of business is to get you back on your medication," Jane had said. "Right after we let your mom and dad know what's going on."

They made that call the following morning. Edith's mom received the news of Jane and Edith's twenty-year reunion with a series of overly polite, soft-toned "oh mys," then took down Jane's number, assuring Jane that Edith's father would call soon from the paper plant where he worked. Moments later, Mr. Mathers' voice spoke through Jane's phone line, every bit as gentle and polite as his wife's had been. Minnesotans.

Jane had been surprised by the ease with which she spoke to both parents. She hadn't been the slightest bit nervous or awkward with either of them. It was as if they discussed Edith's welfare every Tuesday morning. The most pressing issue was the medication, which, Jane discovered, could simply be reintroduced to the girl's system (apparently Edith had gone cold turkey one other time) without adverse side effects.

"Mr. Mathers, I just want you to know that I don't have any delusions about who Edith's real parents are. You and your wife have been with her every step of the way. But I'm really looking forward to getting to know her and hope that you and Mrs. Mathers are okay with that."

"Well, that's very kind of you to say," Mr. Mathers had replied just above a church whisper. "To tell you the truth, Miss Taylor ... "

"Call me Jane," Jane interrupted.

"Jane – I'm just relieved Edith will have someone there to look after her. And of course, we're both so grateful you brought her into our lives. She's been our joy."

With a lump in her throat, Jane had promised to stay in touch, then left the room so Edith could finish the conversation privately.

"He apologized," Edith had confided afterwards. "My dad. He apologized. He said he kept putting off telling me about you because he was afraid of upsetting my mom. He knew I found my birth certificate the moment I brought up going to Harrison, but couldn't seem to mention it to me. I think that was the most honest conversation I've ever had with him."

"That's great, Edith."

"I'm sure he was mostly just afraid of upsetting me. It took a long time to get me on the right dosage of the right medication. I think they were both afraid of throwing me off. You add that to being from Minnesota and not a whole lot of heart-to-hearts are going to be happening."

Jane laughed.

"Thank you," Edith said.

"What did I do?" Jane had asked.

"You made the call. I would have avoided that forever. It's kind of a hobby of mine."

So began the process of Jane and Edith getting to know each other. As their lives returned to their former routines, the two spent hours each day sharing their stories. Edith's included her lifelong struggle with an emotional disorder she didn't understand. Jane's included the revelation that saddened Edith and liberated Jane, the revelation that had ended the show's second episode.

"I'm so sorry," Edith had said before moving across Jane's sofa and giving Jane a hard embrace.

"There's nothing to be sorry about," Jane had replied through tears. "It brought us you."

This last highlight brought a fresh smile to Jane's face as she parked in her customary spot and braced herself for what would surely be a challenging day.

The media had come first. It seemed that every local television station in Pennsylvania, Ohio, and West Virginia converged on Pembrook at the exact same moment, each crew more eager for content than the last one. Band members were the most sought after subjects, but since it was, at its core, a human-interest piece, anybody would do, any human was fair prey for commentary.

Fans came, as well. Ghost Tree had an instant cult following.

Fay was fine with all that. She loved it, in fact. The town's businesses and citizens were blossoming beneath the attention – the more the better in Fay's honest opinion. What Fay wasn't fine with, not by a long shot, was the bombshell that Jane had dropped at the end of last night's show.

Fay hadn't slept. Her phone had been ringing nonstop but she hadn't picked it up once. She wanted to talk to Jane, and Jane alone, about what had been revealed. She stood outside of Steerbucks Tuesday morning like a sentry on watch and rushed to Jane the instant she arrived.

"Hey, Fay – what the heck are you doing here?" Jane asked.

Without a word of warning, Fay wrapped Jane in her strongest, most compassionate bear hug.

"Oh, Janey," she whispered, the palm of her right hand a brush on the back of Jane's hair. "Oh, Janey."

"It's all right, Fay. Really," Jane said as she extricated herself from the woman's clutches. "It's all okay."

Jane unlocked the shop's glass front door and flipped on the lights before leading them back to the counter. Fay took a seat.

"Why didn't you tell me, Jane?" Fay asked. "I could have helped you through that. I could have gone to Pittsburgh with you. You needed somebody who loved you standing beside you through all that."

"I know that, Fay. I know you would have been there for me. I actually thought of calling you from Pittsburgh a bunch of times, but, I don't know, I just seemed to need to be alone. I can't really explain it. It seems like another lifetime now."

Jane continued with the shop's wake-up rituals, shoveling coffee beans, awakening eager machinery, placing the till in the register.

"I know it's ancient history, Jane. It just makes my heart ache to think of what you went through."

Jane stopped what she was doing and stood directly across from Fay. She rested her hand on top of her friend's. "I appreciate that. And I love you for caring. But, as I'm sure you know, the last thing I want is sympathy. That's high on the list of why I didn't say anything back then, I was afraid people would look at me differently, which I'm sure they'll be doing today. I just want to let it all go now … finally. That was the point of the damn interview."

Fay brightened – returning to her natural state of resilience. "Of course you do, honey," she said. "And you should let it go, too. I'm glad you did what you did – the interview, I mean."

At that moment the front door opened and a short, young girl walked in.

"Have you met Edith?" Jane asked as the newcomer reached the counter.

"I don't think I have. Nice to meet you, sweetie."

"Hi," Edith replied.

"You ready for the kicker, Fay?" Jane asked. "Edith is my daughter. She's the reason I disappeared to Pittsburgh."

"Well, I'll be damned," the waitress said, almost speechless but not quite.

Each morning Susan asked herself, "Will this be the day I don't need him inside of me within the first five minutes of my first waking hour?" and each morning the answer was a resounding "No." She rolled off of him now, each of them spent before they'd even taken one foot out of her Cloverleaf bed.

"You better know that I'm more than just a hot bod, dude. I have a mind. I have thoughts."

Kenton laughed. "I know you have thoughts. They just all seem to revolve around the two of us having sex."

"You have a point."

Susan watched as Kenton padded, naked, to the sink. What was it, exactly, that she found so delectably perfect about this man? Maybe it was the fact that his physical parts fit together just right and then they all fit her parts just right. They were like cogs in some perfect little human sex mechanism.

"I love you, Kenton Hall," she said, standing, too. "For your body mostly but a little for your mind."

"I'll take it."

"To conserve water, I'm thinking we should shower together," she said. "You know – for the environment."

As they followed Susan's civic-minded suggestion, forcing their way into the cramped quarters of the dingy shower stall then positioning themselves in such a way that they both received at least some of the nozzle's weak, warm output, Susan said, "How are you feeling about last night?"

"Feels like everything took a shift ... it got all heavy and sad."

"You know we had to do it, Kenton. The music and nostalgia are cool, but the depth will come from the pain and the healing. Then the music will mean even more. Trust me."

"I think I'm just worried about Jane. Seems like a big thing for her to process with a national audience watching."

"Jane will be fine," Susan assured, cupping his dripping face in her dripping hands. "She is a strong person and this will only make her stronger." Damn, did she ever love this man. "And she never would have dealt with it at all if it weren't for us ... if it weren't for you."

"I know. I know."

And she knew that he did.

The kitchen hadn't changed. The same knickknacks sat on the same sun-splashed windowsills. Photographs and post-it notes were attached to the same noisy refrigerator. The dark-green cushioned bench formed an L against the lime-green walls, as they had forever. Mike sat at the table Wednesday morning, comforted by the sameness. He needed the profound feeling of home he still found here. He'd been in a slight funk all week.

It traced back to Monday night when he had viewed the second show with Jane and Edith, at Jane's house. The former priest, the soon to be de-closeted rape victim, and the re-medicating newfound daughter made a strange trio, but their misfit status seemed to bond them.

"You okay, Edith?" Jane had asked as the three sat together following the show's last shot – Jane in the studio after dropping her bombshell. Jane and Mike both moved closer to Edith who sat silently between them on Jane's sofa. "I wouldn't change a thing," Jane reassured. "I swear to God."

The word 'God' had surprised Mike with its power. He rested his hand softly on Edith's shoulder, as she rested her head against Jane. He wanted to be a priest to them both right then, and yet he couldn't do that, be that, any more. He didn't know what brand of comfort to offer and so remained quiet, which was just as well, since the moment belonged to Jane and Edith, not to him.

He remembered it all Thursday morning as he sat at his mom's kitchen table, failing to eat from the breakfast plate she'd prepared for him. Spiritual impotence.

"What's the matter," she asked, "my eggs aren't good enough for you any more?"

They had easily moved past the issue of the disappointment Mike imagined his mother feeling toward him. It turned out he had manufactured that fear out of thin air. She only wanted happiness for her youngest son and would support him wholeheartedly as he pursued it. He forced down a bite of the scrambled eggs.

"I'm sorry, mom, I'm just thinking about Jane and Edith," he said – true, to an extent.

"I've been thinking about Jane myself. How is she?"

"She's actually good. Telling that story has been really healthy for her. She doesn't even seem to be thinking about it too much, except in terms of how it's affecting Edith."

"I can imagine," Mrs. Collins said. "I can't believe she went through all that alone."

"She actually stayed with her dad's sister, I think."

"Well, if she's anything like him, I doubt she was much comfort. What were they thinking, shipping her off to Pittsburgh like that?"

Mike had wondered the same thing himself. And, yet, who was he to judge? He had a heaping helping of his own guilt regarding Jane's 'aloneness' back then.

"Times were different," his mom continued, "but … I don't know. Still feels wrong. Has she talked to them?"

"Yeah. She called to warn them."

"How'd that go?"

"It went okay, I think. I mean it wasn't like they had a teary breakthrough or anything, but Jane felt good talking about it with them. I think part of all this has been her forgiving them for making her feel like the music she was playing had caused what happened to happen. She finally understands she has to let them be them, and try to love them regardless."

"You sound a little like a priest I knew."

"Was he a pompous windbag?"

"More or less."

Mike loved his mom.

"Who would kick whose ass, James Bond or Jason Bourne?"

This question came from Harold Becker, the deliveryman who brought Steerbucks its paper products once a week. He was famous for his ability to get even the grumpiest group talking with questions such as the one he had just posed.

"Bourne," Julie Chetlin answered without hesitation. "In a purely butt-kicking sense, that's a no brainer."

The chatter continued, and Edith smiled as she listened, finally feeling 'normal,' though, of course, she wasn't exactly sure what normal was. Normal for her might have been different than what it was for other people ... normal people. At least she didn't feel like she needed to crawl out of her own skin – which was a nice change.

The time she'd spent with Jane since the parking lot showdown was like medicine to her. In fact, she wasn't sure she was feeling better because she'd resumed taking her pills, or because she was getting to know Jane. Jane Taylor. Her mom.

Edith wouldn't call Jane mom, of course. She already had a mom. But she could tell already that their friendship would feel like the mother-daughter relationships she'd imagined other mothers and daughters having. She could easily picture herself telling Jane secrets, and asking for advice about sex and life, and all of the biggest things.

Edith was happy.

"What are you smiling about?"

Molly asked this upon her return to the counter after a 'pee break.' *Pee break*. Edith would never in a million years say something like that. She liked the funny way Molly had of saying things – bluntness, Edith supposed she would call it.

"Nothing."

"Pull this leg and it plays Jingle Bells," Molly replied.

"Guess I'm just feeling better."

The friends had reconciled shortly after Edith's first new dose of meds. She had apologized profusely to Molly for her erratic behavior, and Molly had forgiven her easily.

Edith reached below the counter and pulled out a yellow rose, which she handed to her freckle-faced co-worker.

"For friendship," Edith said, a little shyly. "Sorry again that I was such a witch."

Molly took the rose and said, "Hey, we all have our bad days. Yours just happened to last a few weeks."

It felt like a planned ceremony Thursday night at the Berg's barn. The four male members of the band were standing in a line when Jane arrived. She went to each of them in turn and gave them long hugs. Jonathon was surprised by how grateful he was for the embrace. He, like everyone in his family and the town, had been stunned in the worst kind of way by the story Jane had told at the end of Monday's show.

"I'm so sorry, Jane," he whispered through her hair as her arms linked tightly behind his back. "I'm so sorry that happened."

With Jane's revelation the mystery was solved – and, in an instant, any resentment he had harbored disappeared and turned into compassion. All he felt now was sweet, brotherly love.

"Guys," Jane said, stepping back from them, "I want to apologize for how I handled everything back then. No matter what I was going through, you guys deserved more. I didn't do anything right."

"I disagree," Mike said. "You had a baby. I'm not sure I can think of anything 'righter' or braver that you could have done."

"I agree with Mike," Jonathon said. "I almost feel like I should apologize to you for the frustration I felt … when you were going through a nightmare. I mean I realize I couldn't have known, but still, I feel bad about it."

"Water under the bridge," Kenny said.

"I was leaving, too," Nathan added. "No matter what you did, Jane, my dad already had me going to the army. My flight to Texas was booked, and there was no way I wasn't going to be on it. So whether you left or not, I was going. Further proof there's nothing to hold on to, regret-wise."

Jane went on to tell them all about her reunion with Edith. "That's why I couldn't rehearse earlier in the week," she explained. "We've been playing catch-up."

Jonathon was amazed at the wonder of God's plan, how intricately it could show itself sometimes. He almost said, "Praise God," as he would have if a similar story were told in his church or on campus at Harrison, but held his tongue. "How awesome is that?" he offered instead.

Jane went on to explain that though Kenton and Susan had agreed to keep Edith out of the show, she knew word would spread quickly, and she wanted them to hear it all from her first. "Here endeth all secrets," she pronounced. "Now let's play some music."

Jonathon felt privileged to witness Jane's joy up close. He was also relieved that Jane had made this meeting a secret one, so there were no cameras running, or producers hovering, or record company executives plotting their next moves.

As he went happily to his station behind the giant Hammond organ, he marveled at the way the band had yet to talk about all that was happening. Though Jonathon had spent many late nights running through all the possibilities with his long-suffering wife, it all became irrelevant when he was with the band playing music. Even the recording sessions had been surprisingly free of the amazement he would have expected from them all, what with their dormant dream suddenly springing to life and all.

But just as their approach to their music was generally wordless, so too was their attitude regarding all that was happening. They just seemed to be flowing with it for now, enjoying it. They were making their first record and rehearsing for their next gig. It was as if no time had passed at all.

Nathan started playing something. Jonathon lost his train of thought, his fingers falling to the organ keys.

Kenton slept and Susan pondered.

The third installment of the show had been delivered hours before. It contrasted the footage from week one's communal screening at the Landmark and accompanying Ghost Tree jam, with the moment from week two's public viewing, when the Landmark crowd learned of Jane's rape. Rock and roll euphoria gave way to stunned silence. The effect was chilling.

Susan reviewed it in her mind now, satisfied that they had brought the themes of the story into focus in a way that remained entertaining even as it dug deeper. The faint strains of *Mystic Light* beneath the end credits had been a harbinger of Jane's, and Pembrook's, healing. At least, to Susan they were.

But there was something else, something Susan couldn't name. It scratched on the wooden lid of her consciousness until finally, just before dawn, it broke through.

Some words.

An image.

She bolted upright in bed and said, "I know who raped Jane Taylor."

Nathan remembered one Sunday when he was thirteen years old, still hovering between boyhood and adolescence. He'd awakened in their house of strangers: his mother and father strangers to him and to each other. He'd dressed, fed himself and left.

The woods were his weekend and summertime refuge. To his childhood sensibility they stretched forever in all directions. He never reached another edge, yet always managed to find his way back to the one through which he'd entered. There were a dozen paths to choose from, and that day he chose the one that led due south, according to the Daniel Boone compass he'd purchased through the mail with cereal box tops. Due south.

He was too old to play the way he did, his imagination still his only friend. He seemed more like a five-year old than a teenager, even using voices to represent the characters in his mind – swashbuckling astronauts navigating Mars' steep ravines and treacherous, rocky landscape, sensing a hostile presence nearby yet persevering nonetheless. Bravely, yet cautiously, he led his side's attack and once victory was secured, commenced exploration. Nature and wildlife, so like earth's and yet so different.

He lost his footing and slid down a particularly steep portion of the woods' decline. The surprise detour brought him to a stand of trees he'd never encountered, and angling between the least-clustered pair, he found himself standing beside a small lake. And though trees towered behind him, the view before him was surprisingly open, the opposite shoreline, maybe thirty feet away, starting a football field sized rectangle of wild grass that led to the horizon, or, more likely, to an interstate his eyes could not detect in the grayness.

The rain came suddenly. Commander Booth stepped back beneath the cover of the long, leafy branches to assess the situation, but his narrative faded as he watched the lines of hard rain pelt this previously unknown portion of the woods. It amazed him that a place so familiar could still surprise him.

When the rain stopped, a rainbow as pronounced and vivid as any Nathan had ever seen formed half a racetrack in the sky, a racetrack that began and ended in the tops of the sideline trees. Nathan had knelt then, his blue-jeaned knees getting soggy in the soft, wet earth. When he finally returned to an upright position, he felt a little lighter than he had before his prayer-like pause.

On a Sunday night a quarter of a century later, Nathan Booth stood before the Ghost Tree in Mischler's field. But in place of the massive Oak before him he saw the secret lake and the racetrack rainbow and, finally, the long walk home from long ago, reality returning with each dread-filled step until he walked through the kitchen door into a horror scene he couldn't say was entirely unexpected.

His father, the fallen military man, was holding Nathan's slight-framed mother from behind. His tattooed arm formed a thick half nelson around her neck. A cigarette glowed between the man's teeth, and, once he'd lifted his wife's bland, brown sweater above her small breasts, he grabbed the burning butt with his fingers and used the end to make a black imprint on her stomach. She screamed in pain.

There were any number of things that could have caused the outburst: cold soup where hot was expected; bread toasted too long; a look that was interpreted as accusing or insulting; a poorly creased pair of work pants. Yet despite the intensity of the sudden storms, they were infrequent, and unrelated to more typical catalysts such as hard liquor. Every now and then, once every three months or so, Nathan's father simply got a taste for rage. After indulging it, he would retreat back to the world of silent disappointment in which he lived.

Before that particular evening, Nathan had always turned away, knowing his turn would come at its random interval. But that time, emboldened perhaps by the beauty he'd just witnessed in the woods, he ran and dove and took his stunned father down, only to be wrestled over easily and marked with the same filter-less Camel branding his mother bore. The black dot had hardened over the years like a second vaccination mark near the top of his right arm.

He touched it now.

In a way, Nathan had been stuck in that memory all of his adult life. It was the reason he'd returned to Pembrook and the reason he stood now before the Ghost Tree on this clear, cool spring night. He needed to forgive them – his father, the cruelty, and his mother the weakness that enabled it – both of them for their inability to give their only child the love he had craved.

"It's okay, Mom and Dad," he whispered to the breeze and the tree and the night itself. "It's okay."

He repeated the phrase over and over.

"It's okay. It's okay. It's okay that you didn't know how to love me or protect me or give me anything close to what a home should be. I forgive you."

And he forgave himself, too, for hating them both and gripping so tightly to the resentment that had become his core belief. It all, finally, fell away.

"I love you, Mom and Dad," he said softly, and meant it for the first time.

The black raven lodged in his heart clawed through blood, tissue, bone, and skin to soar free, washed clean by the air.

Stan Markham drove his rental car from the airport in Pittsburgh to Pembrook where he would remain through Saturday's concert. As he drove, his mind played jazz, thoughts coming in freeform meandering riffs and solos.

He settled for a moment on the touching, incredibly effective way the previous night's show had ended – the Landmark Bar turning from a rock arena to a church in the course of one short, painfully honest interview.

He moved past that feeling of admiration to one of jaded cynicism, quietly deciding that if, in this scandal-addicted day and age, someone says they're shocked by something, they're lying ... or maybe fooling themselves. If it isn't on the cover of USA Today, it's waiting for them in their email inbox, or their Blackberry, or on the giant screens in Time Square. Not only have they seen it before, they've seen it twice – and in high definition.

But there was a time when life moved more slowly. News traveled, but not at the speed of light. He knew that would sound like a parody of someone remembering the 1950s if he were to say it aloud, but that didn't make it any less true. And the 1980s were to his generation what the 1950s were to his parents'. The end of their innocence came with the social upheaval of the 1960s, the end of his came with the technology boom of the 1990s and early 2000s.

That was why the Ghost Tree stuff had hit him so hard, he decided. When he saw the tape of them rehearsing in their barn two decades ago, without a MySpace page, or web site, or a hyper-speed master plan, it took him back to why he fell in love with music in the first place. It took him back to a former version of himself, locked in a bedroom listening to record after record, ten minutes turning

into five hours in four lines of a spot-on chorus or the sound of the
most perfectly unrefined guitar solo he'd ever heard.

Kids today might have a trace of a reaction like that to music
sometimes, but they'd be texting a friend before the song was even
over. And he was that way, too. He'd evolved to the point where he
could never focus on what he was hearing because he was always
wanting the next thing to happen, and in a hurry, before the next
next thing did. He didn't want to miss anything, so he wound up
missing everything.

When Milo sent him the Ghost Tree clip, for some reason, he
slowed down ... and remembered. The look and feel of what he
was seeing sparked it, but the sound of those songs and of Nathan's
voice saw it through.

Stan continued his drive through the gentle morning sunlight
and mentally navigated all that lay ahead of him: the full-length
CD he'd spend the next four days editing and mixing; and the final
Ghost Tree concert, the culmination of everything, Saturday night
in a field beside a tree.

But he kept coming back to the way time collapsed when he was
thirteen years old, sitting alone in his bedroom listening to songs
that painted the world for him. He wanted everyone everywhere
to remember what that felt like ... or to discover it for the first
time.

Dozens of crew members, most recruited from Pittsburgh, had
been working around the clock to transform the Mischler's sloping
green field into a concert venue. Friday morning, Mandy Lomax
stood admiring their progress. The giant stage stood just in front
of the giant tree – so that both the band and its namesake could
easily appear together in a single shot. It was perfect, as were the
elaborate lighting rig and the impressive battery of state-of-the-art
cameras placed strategically according to Mandy's specific instructions. It felt good to be the queen.

"I love the way this is going to look," she said loudly to no one. "Can somebody get me a forecast?"

Weather was the only thing beyond her control, and she thought that by consistently checking it she could force the sky to remain as clear and dry as it had been all week.

"No rain for days," a scruffy, breathless, twenty-something techie called over.

"Fucking perfect," she said to herself, her teeth touching in a childlike smile.

"Mandy," Kenton called from behind as he came up the slight hill to her.

"Hey, Kenton. How awesome is this?"

"Very?"

"Correct," Mandy assured. "It is very awesome. Now we just need thousands of adoring fans to show up."

"If you build it, they will come," Kenton said.

"If you build it, they will come," Mandy echoed, gazing with pride at their temporary Woodtsock. "Where's your woman been hiding?"

"She's chasing down some kind of hunch," he replied. "I decided it was best to steer clear."

"Are you going to come up?"

Jane laughed. She was quoting the scene from *It's a Wonderful Life* in which Mary called down to a pacing and overwrought George Bailey.

"*It's a Wonderful Life?*"

"Yeah," Jane called. "Did your mom tell you to come?"

"Something like that."

"Come on up, dweeb."

As she watched him walk, butterflies the size of small birds appeared in her belly. They hadn't finished the conversation they began in the Landmark parking lot after the first show aired. Jane worried that Mike had started to second-guess his decision to leave the priesthood. She fought the urge to mention it, not wanting to keep him from the choice that would make him the happiest.

"Hey," he said, entering the house as he had a hundred times before. Blue jumped up and down beside them.

"Isn't it past your bed time?" she asked. The clock on the wall read 11:37.

"I'm nervous about tomorrow."

"Me, too," Jane said. "I still can't believe it's happening. Leave it to Chet to get us our biggest gig from beyond the grave."

"I need to talk to you, Jane."

"You really are sounding like George Bailey, Mike. Remember ... when they're listening to that annoying hee-haw guy on the phone together and George gets all crazy. You're freaking me out a little."

"I need to say something," he stammered. "Can I just say something?"

"Say something already."

She was smiling but starting to cry, too. She wasn't exactly sure why.

"I don't regret anything, Jane, because I think I'd die if I started regretting stuff. We all would."

If he knew how ridiculous his angst was, she was sure he'd start laughing. She was tempted to laugh herself but was too busy fighting those damn tears.

"So the fact that I let you down and then chose a path to help me cope with the way I let you down has to be okay..."

Damn, he was handsome. She had never seen a more handsome man.

"God wants us to be happy, Jane. I'm sure of it. He doesn't want for us to suffer or sacrifice or deny ourselves. That's really not the way it works."

She felt like she was expanding with his words and his nervous eyes and his need, his beautiful need. His weight made her weightless.

"Ah, Jane – what I really want to say, what I really need to say, is that I'm in love with you, and always have been, and always will be. That's about the only thing I know for sure. And that's really all I came to tell you. I love you."

She felt as though an angel had entered her lungs and was filling her heart up with holy helium. She felt like it would take work, concentration, to keep herself from floating away. She went public with her tearful laughter and put her hands on his hot cheeks.

"That's really all you came to tell me," she said. "Well let me tell you something."

She pulled his face to hers and kissed him in a way she hoped would erase twenty years of hesitation, turn a friendship into a love affair, and transform all the darkness of all their confusion into bright, white light. She pulled away and held his eyes with hers.

"George Bailey," she said, "I'll love you 'til the day I die."

The sun would be coming up soon, and that was okay with Kenny. Because the sunrise meant a new day, and a new day meant the Ghost Tree concert. And the Ghost Tree concert was pretty much all that Kenny could think about.

He had spent all of his time, awake and asleep, in the studio in Pittsburgh since late Wednesday night. He, Stan Markham, and David Salem had blazed through twelve mixes. Twelve songs that would make up the Ghost Tree debut Kenny was hoping would be named after the band's theme song, *Mystic Light*.

"*Mystic Light,* it is," Stan had announced at the crack of dawn Friday, with the eighth mix safely to bed. "And you, my friend, will get a production credit. We couldn't be doing this without you, Kenny."

The 'this' to which Stan referred was the rampant editing and rearranging so that each song made sense without losing its wild beauty. Kenny intuitively knew where to go at each new musical roadblock. Kenny also understood that the tone and style of Nathan's electric guitar were, in their way, as important to the overall sound of the band as his voice was. They were strands of the same soul.

Kenny listened to the mixes as he drove home to Pembrook early Saturday morning. As each song started he braced himself for sonic remorse. It never came.

He drove and looked at the softly brightening sky, and thought of fundamental things – if not quite timeless, at least enduring. Tires on pavement and hands on a steering wheel; faint morning moons and breaking dawns; windblown songs through open windows – the same now as they ever were.

There were no other cars. He pushed off his headlights so that the changing scene before him was illuminated naturally. He surveyed the hillsides rich with black-green trees and hidden pathways, and thought of the Algonquians or Iroquois who walked them long ago. He thought of his father.

An organ riff jarred him from his reverie.

"Yeah," he screamed to nobody. "We did it!"

Kenny Maxim drummed his steering wheel and sang along to his first record as the sky grew brighter and day began.

10

Shortly after four Saturday morning, Milo was roused from sleep by a knock on his Cloverleaf door. Stan stood bearing a six-pack of Miller Lite, and announced that he had in his possession the 'salvation of rock and roll.' Milo quickly picked up on his friend's excitement and sat eagerly on the edge of the bed, holding his freshly-cracked beer and staring at Stan's little CD player like it was some holy transmitter that would momentarily be broadcasting a message straight from God.

"Jesus Christ," he said after the first song concluded. "This is amazing." Milo couldn't believe how fully realized the sound was … and how completely it evoked the feeling he got seeing Ghost Tree. "Jesus Christ," he said again, track two just starting.

Eventually, with dawn assaulting the drawn blinds, he lay back on his queen-sized bed. Stan did the same in the other. Like carefree college kids they drifted to sleep with empty beer cans on the nightstand and the Ghost Tree disc set to 'repeat.'

It was more dark than light. The window was open, and a breeze blew through the screen. Nathan sat up in his bed. His eyes adjusted to the dimness, and he glanced around the room at the white walls and wooden floor. The simple, eight-note melody continued.

It had begun during the deepest phase of his sleep and lifted him easily to consciousness. It led him now out of his bed and into the adjoining room – a dining room turned recording studio.

Dressed in a white T-shirt and faded red boxer shorts, he lifted his black Martin from its stand. He rested the instrument on his right thigh as he sat and started searching for the dream notes. Once they'd been discovered, he tried laying them in an appropriate bed of chords. As he did so, words came. Actually, just one word: goodbye. He sang over the still-homeless notes and realized that it, and the notes, and the as-yet-unfound chords, were all meant for a piano … a piano he didn't have.

Nathan dressed, grabbed his guitar, and went outside to his truck. By the time he'd made it down the mountain, morning had arrived.

They usually fell to sleep with their hands clasped. Many nights they remained that way until morning. So when the sound of the doorbell – which at first took a place in the sonic landscape of his dreams – awakened Jonathon, his initial reaction was to squeeze his wife's thin fingers together.

"What," she murmured. "What is it?"

"Someone's ringing the doorbell," Jonathon said, standing and grabbing his flannel robe. "If it's a reporter, I think I might shoot him."

"Mmmm … what would Jesus do?"

"I'm pretty sure he'd shoot him, too."

He went downstairs and opened the front door to find Nathan Booth standing there, holding his guitar. It wasn't even in a case.

"Nathan?" Jonathon said. "What the heck are you doing here?"

"I need an assist, man," Nathan said. No apologies for the early hour. No sense of anything even remotely out of the ordinary taking place. "I have this idea for a song, but it has to be on piano. Where's your piano?"

Jonathon led the taller man to his den at the back of the house. An electric keyboard was set up there.

"I was thinking maybe we could end the show with this tonight," Nathan said. "Kind of like U2 used to do with that song *40*. You remember that one?" He lifted his foot onto the room's only chair and started plucking a line on his guitar and singing the word "goodbye" over it.

Jonathon searched for the notes on the piano and played along once he found them. Within moments, a fuller-sounding version began to emerge and Nathan yelled, "Yeah … that's what I was hearing. We need to get everyone together."

"It's not even seven o'clock, Nathan. Don't you think we should wait a while?"

"Hey, Sam," Nathan said to the blushing girl who stood in the doorway, wearing a flannel robe not unlike her father's.

"Hey," she said. "That was pretty."

"Can you call everyone?" Nathan asked Jonathon, completely ignoring the reservation the pianist had just expressed.

"Sure." Jonathon shook his head side-to-side, but was only feigning reluctance. He was actually thrilled to be in action and glad to have this method of killing time between now and their noon load-in. As he made his move for the kitchen phone, he heard Nathan continuing chanting his haunting, "goodbye." The "bye" held over several of the notes, and the voice and guitar clashed in a way that was pure Nathan, pure magic. Jonathon walked faster.

"So that's what all the fuss was about," Mike murmured to no one. He rolled over in Jane's bed to look at the clock. The phone had just awakened them and Jane spoke softly on it now. Mike turned away from the clock and lay quietly, studying her back.

"We'll be there," Jane said before hanging up the receiver.

"We'll be where?"

"I think I just gave poor Jonathon a heart attack," Jane said. "I let it slip that you were here with me. And I'm pretty sure he heard sin in my voice. Hope you don't mind."

Mike smiled then laughed, picturing Jonathon struggling to incorporate such a tidbit into his reality. "I love Jonathon," he said. "Where are we meeting him?"

"Up on campus ... at the Fine Arts center. Nathan has a new song, and Jonathon loves the piano there."

Jane fell back onto the mattress and they stared at the ceiling. "How are you feeling, Mike?" she asked. "Any regrets?"

"My only regret is that I waited until I was thirty-eight to experience the wonders of Jane Taylor."

"You're not going to be needing to sow your wild oats or anything like that, are you? If there's one thing I can't stand it's a promiscuous ex-priest."

"I should be okay," he said. "You just might not be getting much sleep for a while." He leaned up on his elbow and studied the parts of her that were showing, then leaned down and kissed a shoulder. "Thanks for showing me the way last night," he said, momentarily pausing his morning worship.

"Are you kidding me? Thank you for giving me twenty years of your pent-up sexual energy. My experience isn't exactly vast in this area, but I'm pretty sure you show real potential." She rested her hand on his shoulder. "Don't let it go to your head. Either of them."

"I'm just a humble student," Mike said and eased up onto her again.

"Top of the morning," she sighed in a soft, silly brogue.

Kenny was the last arrival to Pew Auditorium, the most modern-looking building on the campus of Harrison College with its abundance of glass and cut angles. He'd been summoned on his cell phone a half-hour before, effectively eliminating any possibility of sleep. Kenny didn't care – though he still wasn't sure what they were doing there. He grabbed a conga drum from the back of his van just to be safe.

Jonathon fumbled with some keys, then slid one into the clear front door. In single file, the groggy group followed its redheaded leader through the lobby and into a good-sized concert hall that Kenny guessed could hold one thousand people. "This place is sweet," he said.

"Cost enough," Jonathon replied.

Jonathon reached the grand piano and sat. Nathan, carrying a beautiful, black acoustic guitar, joined him there, facing the rest of the group from the end of the bench. Kenny sat on the stage and gripped his drum between his thighs. Jane and Mike followed suit. They looked like kindergartners on a field trip.

"Thanks for doing this everybody," Nathan said. "I had an idea this morning and thought it might be a cool last song tonight. Tell me if I'm crazy."

Jonathon played a slow progression of four chords as Nathan picked a melody Kenny had trouble hearing. Nathan started to sing in his highest, most feminine voice, sounding almost angelic.

Kenny noticed a change in Mike and Jane. They seemed different. Together. He also sensed that the single word Nathan sang over and over in his high, thin, angel voice, signaled another ending for the band and knew that Ghost Tree would not be touring the country or the world any time soon.

Without even knowing he was doing it, Kenny started beating on the conga. Mike and Jane found harmonies and sang along with Nathan. It was beautiful. As they went on and on with their one-word encore Kenny grinned, aware that everything was exactly as it should be and that this was the only 'band meeting' they would ever need to have.

"I have something I need to play for you guys," Kenny said as they emerged from Pew into the still-fresh morning. "Who's up for a drive?"

"Let's do it," Jane said – yelled, really – though what she actually wanted to do was get back to her house, to her bed, and continue to make up for lost Mike time – a life-long endeavor, but one to which she felt equal. She grabbed Mike's hand and led them in a run to Kenny's battered old VW Bus. "You should really think about some new wheels, Kenny. Like maybe a K Car or something, just to move a little bit toward the present day."

She opened the unlocked back door and took a seat by the driver-side window. Mike slid in beside her and Nathan beside him. Jonathon took the front passenger seat. As Kenny reached for the radio Jane called, "Wait. Let's drive through McDonalds and get coffee first. All those in agreement say aye."

"Aye," the men said in unison. Five minutes later, once they all had giant coffees in their possession, Kenny lifted the disc and announced, "Lady and gentlemen – Ghost Tree's long-awaited debut."

Sunlight dappled the van's powder blue interior. Mike's arm was warm against Jane's. She leaned against it for support. The music spilled out of the speakers. Jane found it difficult to place herself within it, to understand that she was a co-creator, but soon gave up trying, surrendering to the massive sound, larger than all of them.

Song after song, they remained suspended in their moving minibus with the scenery of their youth, their lives, passing easily outside the window. Jane quietly laid claim to all the moments of her past, especially those created in that golden summer, twenty years before. She also held tightly to the more recent ones, the ones of the past twelve days and those of the past twelve hours, in which new worlds had opened, and she had finally moved beyond her boundaries and allowed herself to feel the promise of joy, the promise of love, the promise of summer.

At high noon, a loud knock at the door awakened Milo from a deep sleep. He jumped out of bed and rushed to answer it.

"You guys aren't going gay on me are you?" Susan asked before commenting on Milo's silk-boxers-plain-white-t ensemble, then announcing, "We need to talk, Milo."

Stan roused himself and embarked on a slightly disconcerting throat-clearing procedure that lasted a good thirty seconds.

"You okay there buddy?" Susan asked.

"What? Yeah. Sure." He nodded toward the dresser top sound system. "Hear that, Susan? Rock and roll's salvation."

"Jesus Christ," she said. "That sounds amazing."

"So what's up?" Milo asked.

Susan sat down on the room's lone chair. "First of all, I figured out who raped Jane Taylor."

"Jesus, Susan," Milo said. "How the hell'd you manage that?"

She told them the story of the past twenty-four hours. "Of course, it happened twenty years ago and Jane never pressed charges or anything, so there's not a whole lot we can do about it."

"Then why do I feel like you still have a plan?" Milo asked.

"Because I do," she replied. "But I'll need your help."

Ghost Tree music streamed from open windows.

"How do people have the songs already?" Edith asked.

"This is crazy," Molly said as she and Edith walked beside highway 29, which looked like a parking lot with its bumper-to-bumper, barely-moving traffic. "Where will they all park?"

"Jane said they turned half of the field into a parking lot and the other half into a music venue. I think they're also bussing people from the high school parking lot, which might help a little."

It was so good to have Edith back, Molly thought. Though Edith was naturally quiet, she had a shy sense of humor that perfectly complemented Molly's more extroverted brand. For a few days there, though, there had been no sign of the girl Molly had gotten to know over the course of the school year. Edith had become one of those people you hope won't sit beside you on public transportation – stammering to herself and sprouting twitches. If things hadn't changed exactly when they did, Molly would have gone to Jane herself. She was relieved that hadn't had to happen.

"Can you believe all this, Edith? How cool it is that we're walking to a Ghost Tree concert? This is like your dream come true, right?"

Edith smiled in answer.

"I'm glad you're back," Molly said as they arrived at the edge of the field, which was already filling with people even though Ghost Tree wouldn't hit the stage for another five hours.

"Me, too," Edith agreed.

They saw Fay seated on a lawn chair sipping from a can of beer and claimed a neighboring patch of territory.

"Can you believe this?" the friendly waitress asked. "Where will they all sleep?"

A fifteen-passenger white Dodge Ram picked up each band member, starting with Nathan and ending with Jane and Mike, and drove them along their secret route down the Mischeler's driveway and through the top end of the field.

"Holy shit," Jane said, beholding the standing throng of people as they slowly covered the distance to the tent that had been set up for them behind the stage.

The others just looked on in wonder.

"Holy shit," Jane repeated.

"Holy shit," Mike said finally. "Is that what you're needing? For someone else to say holy shit?"

"Yes. Thanks."

"Holy shit," Nathan said, too.

"Holy shit," Jonathon and Kenny added.

They walked directly from the van into the tent where they found the members of the Dan Finbar Band. Jane had made sure her old friend was given the opening slot.

The merged musical outfits hovered near the catering table making small talk, until Mandy popped her head into the tent and announced "Time to get out there, Fin."

"Break a leg," Jane called, suddenly fighting a surge of nerves. She pulled Mike closer, the wind knocked out of her by how good it felt touching her friend like the lover he'd become.

According to the legend, the spirits of those from the town who had died with secrets or sins were held here, within this tree, until some resolution had been offered, some forgiveness or understanding granted. Kenny Maxim was surprised by the strong, sudden impulse he felt to stand there now and speak with his father as Finbar and his band played.

"Hey dad," he said. "You're probably not here. I don't think you had any big secrets." His yellow mop of hair fell forward as he pushed the massive tree trunk with his long, thin arms – part of a pre-show stretching ritual – then returned to an upright position. "I hope you are here, though, dad. I think you might have been our biggest fan."

A breeze rustled the leaves.

"I never really told you how much that meant to me. You loving Ghost Tree. You being so proud of my drumming ... like I was the star of the football team or something."

He backed away to look at the tree in its entirety. Finbar's rich baritone floated through the darkening night.

"Thank you. Maybe you're still here waiting to hear me say that, since I never got around to saying it when you were alive. Thank you for being such a good dad and for never trying to push me onto a different path, or caring that I didn't want to go to college, or do anything other than play music." He paused, then added, "And for being such a rock for me when mom left."

He stretched his arms and looked up at the sky. "I love you, dad. This show's for you."

He returned to the tent, anxious for the biggest performance of his life to be underway.

"Is he awesome or what?" she asked.

Mike watched Jane watch Finbar. "Easy there, Sparky. You have a boyfriend."

"Finbar's a brother for life, dude. You're just a passing phase."

Mike resisted the urge to rebut and listened to Finbar singing his last song, one about being lost in America.

"Grace is everywhere," he thought, beginning to write a homily he'd never deliver. The kernel of his idea got blown away in a strong gust of wind. He sang along to the chorus and reached for Jane's hand.

As the Dan Finbar Band left the stage, a light rain began to fall. Far from being upset, Stan knew that it was as perfect as everything else had been. And though he wasn't religious, he couldn't shake the sense that Ghost Tree's surge to stardom was sanctioned by heaven. The light rain that fell now was cleansing history of its sin of omission where Ghost Tree was concerned.

Stan had spent the afternoon with Milo seeing to last-minute details and assisting with Susan's bold plan, but had wandered off as show time approached. He always preferred to watch concerts alone. He liked to become anonymous, to turn himself into a blank slate for the music, before merging with the crowd as it – as they – became one thing, one being, one spirit.

Stan Markham jogged in place. He took the band from his pony-tail and shook his gray-peppered black hair free. He leaned back, opened his arms, and felt the rain upon his face. He waited for the music to begin.

Kenton forgot that he had fallen in love with Susan Clawson. He forgot that he had masterminded the event he now witnessed. He forgot that he had lived twenty years since the last Ghost Tree concert and that he had traveled and changed, struggled and thrived. He forgot that he was supposed to be using the camera he held to capture the energy from here in the heart of the crowd, so that Mandy would be able to maintain the ruddy character of the show as she cut together the night's footage. He forgot that Jane Taylor had been raped and that her grown daughter, Edith, stood next to him in the overcrowded field.

As the stage went dark and Ghost Tree emerged, Kenton forgot everything. He was twelve years old again, standing on tiptoes by the side of Berg's barn, breathless with anticipation. And with the first electric chimes of the first song, he was transported out of himself into the same, vast world of possibility. As Nathan started singing, Kenton, Edith, and Molly pushed toward the stage.

Shannon Sax screamed at the top of her lungs. Her jumping up and down gave the scream a siren-like, in-motion quality that Samantha Hilliard would have found annoying, if she weren't so busy screaming herself. The band had just ripped into *She Took the Key*, causing the already frenzied crowd to kick it up a notch, shifting into whirling-dervish mode.

At first, Sam's friends had been reluctant to jump aboard the Ghost Tree train – it being run, at least partially, by the dorky dad of one of their own. There was an unwritten law: parents were fundamentally uncool ... though they could, on occasion, be of service. All bets were off once the girls heard Nathan's voice, though. And the visual accompaniment that came courtesy of YouTube, then CBS, sealed the deal. The man was hot. And, Sam assured them, he was available.

"I love you," Carmella Craver bellowed.

Samantha sang along to the song and felt, for a moment, like she might just start to fly.

In warrior mode, Mandy battled the hordes to get the shots that she needed: Samantha Hilliard and her friends dancing; Mike Collins' mother, brother and sister-in-law staring at the stage in loving wonder; Old John and Fay, whom Susan had managed to force together in a safe, slightly out-of-the-way location, smiling at the carnival. But the images that really captivated Mandy were of all those she didn't know – strangers lost to these songs.

"How could this happen so quickly?" she wondered. "Was it the power of television, the Internet, or the music?"

She allowed herself a moment to stop and listen, to look with them instead of at them. She recognized the song, of course. It was the one the band had written at their first rehearsal – *Never Thought*. Is that what they had decided to call it? Whatever it was called, Mandy loved it. And as she drummed her thigh with an opened right hand she knew the answer to her question was 'c' – the music. The music was the reason for all of this.

Reluctantly, she returned the lens of the camera to her right eye and continued her documentary-making.

The crowd looked like an ocean, an ocean with ten thousand faces. It was Strawberry Days times twenty, a rock and roll fantasy come true. Jonathon searched and searched and finally found Sam standing dead center, about twenty feet from the stage. He watched in awe as his beautiful daughter danced with an abandon he hadn't seen from her since she was a toddler.

"Praise God," he thought, overwhelmed by an urge to be standing out there with her and not up on the stage. The urge faded, though, when the chorus started.

Mystic Light evolved from a waltzing ballad to a punk Irish rave and lasted more than twelve minutes. Nathan watched as the rain and light joined to bathe the crowd in pure holiness. He drank in the sight as he sang, Jane's voice blending with his on the second chorus before Jonathon overtook them both with a jarring, jagged, wonderful Hammond solo.

It had all gone the way he had hoped it would – every last thing. He looked past Jonathon at the Tree and watched as the once-tortured spirits of his parents ascended from the leaves, lifted by the wind, free at last.

"Free at last, free at last," he sang into the vacuum of sound that filled the brightly colored stage. Lifting his sights from the tree to the sky he sang it some more, "Free at last, free at last, free at last…"

His eyes met Jane's, and her smile assured him that she knew, too.

They'd been brushing arms all night. As Ghost Tree's beautiful encore concluded, Edith realized that though the music had been perfect and that seeing Jane shining from the stage like some rock star supernova had blown Edith away, what was really lighting up her switchboard was Molly's arm and all the brushing up against hers it kept doing. As Nathan Booth sang his last "Goodbye," she sensed that Molly, too, was noticing the arm-connection. It became more of a goal than an accident.

The rain fell harder as the crowd cheered. Edith and Molly turned toward each other, and there was little doubt what would happen next. The two friends kissed for as long as their racing hearts could stand it.

Susan stood back farther than anyone else. She knew that Mandy was frantically capturing every moment that she possibly could, and that Kenton was somewhere close to the stage being a twelve-year old, but she needed a moment to herself and retreated. The last song was ending. One by one the band members left the stage though the audience showed no sign of following suit, singing loudly as the music dissipated, already claiming the song for themselves.

Susan decided in that moment, with Nathan's one-word mantra reverberating through the open field, that she didn't want to go back to the life she had known prior to this experience. It wasn't a bad life, by any means, but she liked this one better. She wanted to preserve the paradise she and Kenton had discovered in their Cloverleaf Motel room.

She scanned the mass of humanity before her, and took a moment to feel proud of what they had accomplished. They had resurrected a band as deserving of resurrection as any band had ever been. They had helped Jane Taylor to finally stare down her past, own her pain, and then give it away. They had even aided in the reunion of a mother and a child. And maybe best of all, they had displayed an aspect of the American past that was worth clinging to – innocence, in the form of a small Pennsylvania town, and the magical songs of a magical band.

She made her way backstage where she found Jane and the guys still basking in the concert glow. She hugged each of them, ending with Jane.

"Can we talk?" she asked the smiling, beautiful guitar player.

"Sure," Jane replied.

Larry Terk had a tried and true technique for getting drunk on a budget. He'd make a show of buying the first few rounds early, when the crowd was still thin. This opening volley always seemed to create a flow of good will that enabled him to drink free for the remainder of the night and get him to the numb, fuzzy place he liked so well.

The night of the final Ghost Tree broadcast, he sat on his customary stool with a battery of shots and beers lined up before him – his system working to perfection. He felt the crowd swell behind him, the buzz growing louder as the 9:00 hour approached.

"Shut the hell up everybody," Pete screamed from behind the bar. "It's starting!"

"Be my priest." Late, late Sunday night, Jane had whispered those words as she and Mike sat side by side on her front porch swing. "I don't know what to do, Mike. Give me counsel. Guide me through."

She'd been surprised by the way it felt when he took her hands in his and prayed. It wasn't like she remembered from her childhood, when all the words had seemed so forced and false. Mike spoke as if God were their most trusted and loyal friend. His words seemed to spring directly from his heart … and her heart, too.

She stood now in the ladies room of the Landmark Bar, awaiting her cue and gathering her courage. Soon she would join Susan in the back where Susan's scheme would play out. Jane hoped she had the guts to speak the words that had come to her the night before, as she sat with Mike in the quiet stillness, praying.

On televisions throughout America and the world, the concluding segment of the fourth and final Ghost Tree installment would feature an eloquent little speech Susan wrote, summing up their Ghost Tree journey and thanking all the people who had made Chet Howard's dying wish come true.

In the back room of the Landmark Bar, however, a much different ending would be playing – an ending Susan, Mandy, Kenton and Milo had created for an audience of one.

"Here we go," Susan said.

She left Kenton's side and made her way to the bar.

"Hi Larry," Susan whispered directly into Larry Terk's left ear.

He felt her breath on his skin. It was the closest thing to female contact he'd had in years, and it sent a shiver down his spine. He couldn't say he was completely surprised, though. They'd been pretty friendly when Susan dropped by the bar a few days before.

"Hello, pretty lady. Back for some more?"

"Actually, Larry, I was wondering if you would join me in the back room to watch the last part of the show. I have a surprise for you."

"I guess Christmas is here early," he replied, standing with a wobble. "Lead the way." He grabbed his beer and followed as she led him to a small, back room. The only light came from a television that sat on a desk. There were two empty chairs placed before it. "Our own private theater," Larry slurred. "I like it."

Susan sat and Larry sat beside her just as a commercial ended. Susan's televised image peered out at them. "Look at you," he barked.

"Just keep watching, Larry."

> *(On the screen, Susan walks through the Mischler's field then comes to a stop. The Ghost Tree looms behind her.)*

Susan: The past is a tricky thing. We tend to make it out to be either worse or better than it actually was; we're all historical revisionists to some extent. In the case of Ghost Tree, though, it seems that the recollections of all those involved weren't inflated ... it actually was magic and still is. I am forever grateful to have been here to witness it first hand. Before signing off, though, I'd like to take a minute to tie up a few loose ends.

      We talked with Jane Taylor off-camera and she gave us permission to tell you something we haven't included in the broadcasts. In the course of the making of this show, the daughter Jane gave up for adoption twenty years ago re-entered her life, and the two have begun the process of getting to know one another. It's a beautiful thing. I've met the girl. She has Jane's eyes.

Also, over the course of these broadcasts, something occurred to me. It was after the airing of episode two. As we were reviewing the footage, a face in the crowd at the Landmark Bar caught my eye. It was the face of Larry Terk. If you can't place Larry, we'll refresh your memory. *(The initial clip of Larry plays – the one in which he describes running into Jane and offering comfort.)*

"What the hell?" Larry blurted. He squirmed in his seat.

"Keep watching," Susan commanded. "Just keep watching."

Susan: The thing that was gnawing at me was Larry's mention of Jane's bike. In the interview where Jane described the attack, she said that was the only time all summer she rode her bike to rehearsal. Normally, she caught a lift with Mike, but he was leaving early, so she went with the bike.

I went to Jane and asked if she remembered seeing anyone near the Berg's that night after the attack and she said no. The rapist left her there ... and when she was able, she walked her bike home, alone.

Next, I went to the bar and had a few off-camera beers with Larry. In the course of small talk, I asked him if he had ever known Jane Taylor in the Biblical sense. He said no. Actually, his exact words were, "She has a nice little body on her, but I never had the pleasure of experiencing it."

Larry looked at the door over his shoulder. He considered running.

Susan placed her hand on his forearm.

"Almost there," she said.

Susan: When Larry excused himself, I placed one of his empties, a bottle from which he had sipped repeatedly, into a plastic bag, like I've seen actors do in police dramas. With the help of executives at CBS and a crime lab in Pittsburgh, and with the knowledge and consent of Jane and the child she delivered twenty years ago, we were able to determine something – something hard and painful, something which will be the last chapter of this remarkable story as it marks the start of many happier ones.

       Larry Terk, the bar stool philosopher, the harmless town drunk, raped Jane Taylor on a summer night twenty years ago. Larry has spent the past two decades rewriting history; transforming himself from the rapist he was into a gallant, concerned citizen who did nothing more than offer assistance to a young girl in trouble. Time to settle your tab and face the music, Larry.

The room light came on and the door opened. Jane Taylor stood in the doorway.

"It was twenty years ago," Larry offered weakly.

"Not for me, Larry," Jane said softly. "For me it was yesterday."

"But... but... "

"You don't need to say anything," Jane said. "I'll do the talking." She took a step closer. Her eyes remained leveled on the sad, pathetic man. "I don't know why you did the terrible thing you did to me. I can only imagine you must have been in a dark, lonely place to have hurt me that way."

She moved closer, just a few feet away from him now. "I get the sense that you've punished yourself more than any prison ever could have. And I want you to know that ... I forgive you." A tear rolled down Jane's cheek.

Larry suddenly crumbled into the broken man he was. His body convulsed as he sobbed and shook. Jane leaned down and laid a hand on his shoulder.

"It's okay," she whispered. "I forgive you. I forgive you."

Larry stood and staggered from the room.

With a teary smile, Jane looked at Susan. "Think he knows that was his own special edit of the show?"

"He doesn't have a clue," Susan replied.

Nathan sipped his water and looked around.

Mandy, Kenton, Susan and Milo were there. Jon and Kenny were, too. Mike had called all the band members that afternoon to tell them what was happening and enlist their moral support. Each had come running, figuratively speaking.

"Who's buying?" Susan called.

Milo waved the network credit card in the air. "That would be me," he replied.

Mike whispered into Jane's ear. Whatever he said made her smile, then laugh.

Jon and Kenny talked to some fans.

Nathan's mind wandered.

He thought about Larry Terk.

He thought about his father.

He thought about people in general, failings and secrets, mountains to climb.

He thought about the small, true place in each of us where divinity hides – too well, most of the time.

Finally, Nathan thought about the beautiful gift Jane had given them all in that dingy backroom just a short while ago: a lesson in the only thing that really mattered, forgiveness.

Humming a song, he set down his water and walked out the door.

Epilogue

After Edith and Molly had 'come out' to themselves, they came out to the world at large. And though a small town like Pembrook and a conservative college like Harrison are not exactly lesbian sanctuaries, the school year wasn't as difficult as the girls might have predicted. Beyond the occasional mercy call from a concerned student who, though not judging, was prayerfully concerned over their salvation, they were pretty much left alone, which was fine by them.

When Jane revealed who Edith's real father was, it became a running joke between Molly and Edith. Whenever Edith was being a bitch, Molly would say something like "Your boozehound rapist side is showing through, E," or "Stop being such a drunken assailant for God's sake." And though the comedy was on the dark side, it helped Edith process things. Not that she felt the need for too much processing. As far as Edith was concerned, she already had a mom and dad. Jane was like a super-cool Godmother who filled in Edith's empty spaces, and whom Edith absolutely loved to be around. Larry Terk didn't really factor into it, though she suspected her 'mood struggles' descended from the scrawny bastard.

And now, one year later, Edith stood by Kenton Hall in Mischler's field among the massive crowd that had gathered for Ghost Tree's second annual reunion concert. The band had decided that rather than uprooting their lives and doing the tour Columbia had hoped they would do, they'd play just once a year by the tree that inspired their name.

Sales of their CD were in excess of thirteen million copies worldwide, and they were all in the process of becoming rich. Jane had used her 'take' to purchase Steerbucks from Harry Compton. It was now officially called 'Jane's Place' (though she vowed to maintain the psycho cowboy motif she loved so dearly.)

So far, Jonathon had funneled his earnings into college funds for his kids, but was considering early retirement and eyeing the massive Winnebago on sale at Howard's Auto.

Kenny Maxim had taken up residence in New York City, where he was in high demand as an up-and-coming producer, thanks in large part, to Stan Markham. Mike Collins' lone purchase thus far had been the diamond ring he offered to Jane over Christmas as part of a marriage proposal. The wedding was scheduled for early August.

Nathan, of course, had made no purchases that anyone knew of. To the contrary, he had sold his mountain home to Kenton and Susan, and returned to California where he was continuing his spiritual studies. Kenton and Susan, in the meantime, formed a production company that, in addition to movies and television shows, apparently included human life. Susan was five months pregnant and looking absolutely radiant.

All of this information trickled down to Edith through Jane, for whom she still worked and with whom she shared at least three meals a week. Edith smiled now, noticing the glint of Jane's engagement ring in the stage lights.

"Things have a way of working out."

Was that the way Old John had put it to her the afternoon before? However he'd worded it, Edith couldn't agree more. Things had certainly worked out.

"How do they do it?" Kenton asked. "How do they sound so amazing when they haven't played together in a year?"

Ghost Tree had just finished the last song of their set.

"I made it up, Kenton," Edith blurted.

"What?"

"I made it up."

"What did you make up?" Kenton continued his clapping but glanced at Edith.

"I made up the whole 'death-bed-reunite-the-band' thing," she said.

"You what?" he asked, turning to her with a confused look on his face.

""Actually, I wrote it up and had Molly play the part. She was lying through her teeth when she went to talk to Mike that first time." She searched his face for signs of anger but saw only curiosity. "I found a few newspaper clippings and articles about the band. I knew who the members were ... and who their manager was. Molly was volunteering at the hospital when Chet Howard came in. She mentioned his name and I seized the opportunity. I thought maybe my real father was in the band. And I just wanted to see them play."

A stagehand ran out to adjust something – a sure sign that more music was coming. The murmuring crowd grew louder.

"Are you kidding me, Edith?"

"No," she said, "I'm not. Are you mad?"

"No."

A smile broke across his face. It occurred to Edith that though she'd spent a decent amount of time with Kenton over the past year (Kenton and Susan were frequent dinner guests at Jane and Mike's) this was the first undeniable smile she had seen from him. She liked it. It inspired a smile of her own.

"Our secret?" she asked.

"Our secret."

They laughed and then yelled as Ghost Tree returned to the stage.

When he's not churning out novels, Bill Deasy is busy writing and recording songs and then singing them for anyone who will listen. He lives with his wife and sons in Oakmont, Pennsylvania.

Thanks to my team of critical readers: Art Edwards, Bill Deasy (my dad, not me,) A.J. and Paula. Thanks also to Holly Ollivander and Huw Thomas for being such stellar allies.

LaVergne, TN USA
08 December 2010
207858LV00001B/18/P